Three Wives' Tales

Basque originals, 28

THREE WIVES' TALES

Dale Erquiaga

Center for Basque Studies
University of Nevada, Reno
2021

Three Wives Tales
Basque Originals No. 28

Center for Basque Studies University of Nevada, Reno
1664 North Virginia St, Reno, Nevada 89557 usa
http://basque.unr.edu

Library of Congress Cataloging-in-Publication Data

Names: Erquiaga, Dale, author.
Title: Three wives' tales / Dale Erquiaga.
Description: Reno : Center for Basque Studies Press/University of
Nevada,
   Reno, 2021. | Series: Basque originals ; 26
Identifiers: LCCN 2021055520 | ISBN 9781949805598
(paperback)
Subjects: LCSH: Erquiaga, Dale--Family--Fiction. | Basque
   Americans--Fiction. | LCGFT: Biographical fiction. | Novels.
Classification: LCC PS3605.R8523 T48 2021 | DDC 813/.6--dc23/
eng/20211203
LC record available at https://lccn.loc.gov/2021055520

Contents

For my mother, the person I knew and loved,
and the person she might have been.

Introduction & Acknowledgements

In my family, stories were like currency. Your social standing within the clan depended on how good a storyteller you were. Holidays, picnics, visits from the extended relatives—all of these were opportunities to tell a story. My paternal grandfather was the champion; even with no formal English education, his tales of coming to America from Spain were the stuff of legend. My aunts and uncles could also spin a good yarn, some better than others, and any time liquor flowed, laughter was sure to follow. As a child, I soaked it up (the storytelling, not the liquor).

I later realized that my family told stories for two reasons. The first was sheer entertainment. We were poor, truth be told, and stories were free. But a second reason for the endless recitation of tales from the Old Country and life during the Great Depression was, I now understand, a desire to keep their traditions alive. History mattered. Context mattered. Being Basque mattered. We weren't like other people, and on some level the more we *became* like other people—the more "American" we became—the more important it was to remember where we came from.

Beginning in the 1980s, my mother and her sister, my Aunt Jessie, became enamored with genealogical research. They started by transcribing an oral history my uncle had dictated before his death, then moved on to researching ship manifests, birth and death certificates, and newspaper articles gleaned from microfilm at the public library. And they wrote stories. Neither had more than a high school education, but both were good storytellers and quite good writers. Over the period of about 15 years, they recorded everything they could remember about our family's experiences in Spain and Nevada in the twentieth century. When their own recollections failed them, they interviewed their siblings and in-laws, committing everything to paper via electric typewriters.

Eventually, my mother upgraded to a word processor and began to write a short first-person memoir about her life. She called the story "Annie," a name from childhood that I never heard anyone else use, but which she seemed to remember quite fondly. My mother fussed with her story for years, while she and Aunt Jessie compiled binders of records, photographs, and third-person narratives. Somewhere along the way, Mom began to tell me, "You're going to have to do something with all these stories. We're counting on you."

That "something" became this book. This is a work of historical fiction and personal memoir, based on the stories my family told and my mother's writings. I found it impossible to change Annie's story from the first person, so you will read many of her own words. I have taken some literary license to add content that advanced her narrative (the suggestion she run for political office never occurred, to my knowledge) or to reveal emotions she confided to me or which I have inferred.

The stories of my grandmothers, Victoria and Eladia, contain historical fact, personal memories, and—occasionally—pure fiction that I have added to the tale, either to help me understand sometimes complicated people or simply because I, too, like to tell a good story. I'm sure there are people who remember these events differently or members of my family who will not like how I have portrayed our ancestors. I hope they will forgive me.

With few exceptions, the people in this book are/were real. In some cases, I have omitted the surnames of people outside my family. And except for Eladia's rather glamorous life before meeting my grandfather—all of which is a product of my imagination—most of these events happened, or at least they are *remembered* to have happened. I've learned a good deal about the nuances of how we remember events as I visited the highways and byways of my family's journey.

The reader should keep in mind that my family did not speak English at home for many years after coming to America. Dialogue in the chapters about Victoria would have occurred primarily in Basque; dialogue in Eladia's chapters would have been in Spanish. However, for the reading comfort of an American audience—and, let's be honest, since I have virtually no facility with either of my ancestral tongues—everything is written in English, and only on rare occasions do I resort to phonetically depicting accents.

This book would not have been possible without some dear friends: Dana Bennett, who taught me that the stories of women aren't told nearly enough; Denice Miller, who edited and encouraged, reminding me that "he nodded silently" is just bad writing; my former colleagues at Communities In Schools, who pushed me to spend the 2020 pandemic lockdown writing; Keith Weaver, who provided details of the ties that have bound our families together for 80 years; and Dr. Sandy Ott, who suggested I enter the Basque Literary Contest sponsored by the University of Nevada, Reno and Boise State University, an act which ultimately led to the publication of this book. Special thanks to my brother, Steve, and my niece, Allison, the first family members to give their blessings to early drafts. And to my sixth-grade teacher, Miss Dawn Cassinelli, who was the first person who told me I could be a writer.

But most importantly, this book would not have been possible without the many storytellers of the Rubianes and Erquiaga families. I hope it lives up to their standards. And I hope my children and grandchildren, and my many nieces and nephews, remember with pride the tales of three Basque wives who lived simple but inspiring lives. Because that legacy was the whole point of writing this tale.

Dale Alan Rubianes Erquiaga
Las Vegas, Nevada
March 2021

(Family tree of Antonio and Maria Carmen Urrutibeascoa, Victoria's parents)

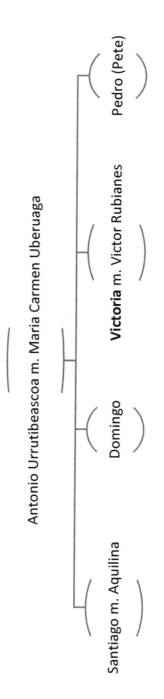

Antonio Urrutibeascoa m. Maria Carmen Uberuaga

Santiago m. Aquilina

Domingo

Victoria m. Victor Rubianes

Pedro (Pete)

(Family tree of Manuel and Emeteria Rubianes, Victor's parents and Victoria's in-laws)

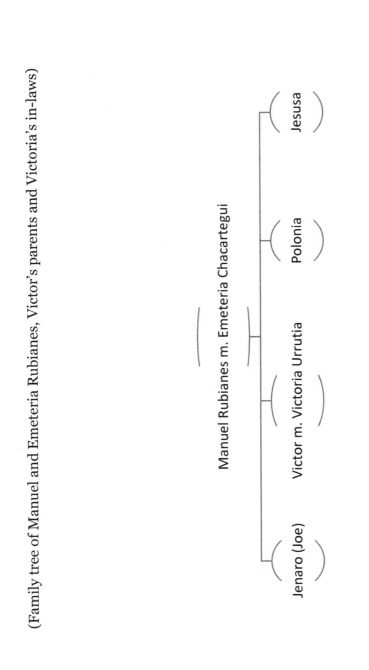

Manuel Rubianes m. Emeteria Chacartegui

Jenaro (Joe)   Victor m. Victoria Urrutia   Polonia   Jesusa

(Family tree of Nicanor and Francisca Aguirre, Eladia's parents)

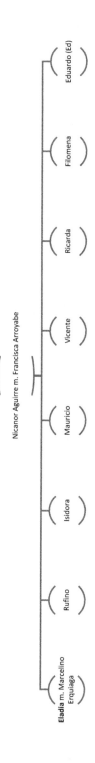

Nicanor Aguirre m. Francisca Arroyabe

Eladia m. Marcelino Erquiaga

Rufino

Isidora

Mauricio

Vicente

Ricarda

Filomena

Eduardo (Ed)

(Family tree of Domingo and Monica Erquiaga, Marcelino's parents and Eladia's in-laws)

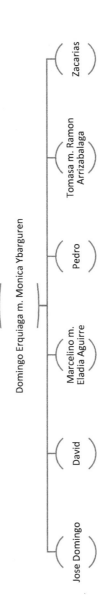

Domingo Erquiaga m. Monica Ybarguren

Jose Domingo

David

Marcelino m.
Eladia Aguirre

Pedro

Tomasa m. Ramon
Arrizabalaga

Zacarias

(Family tree of Victor and Victoria Rubianes, Annie's parents)

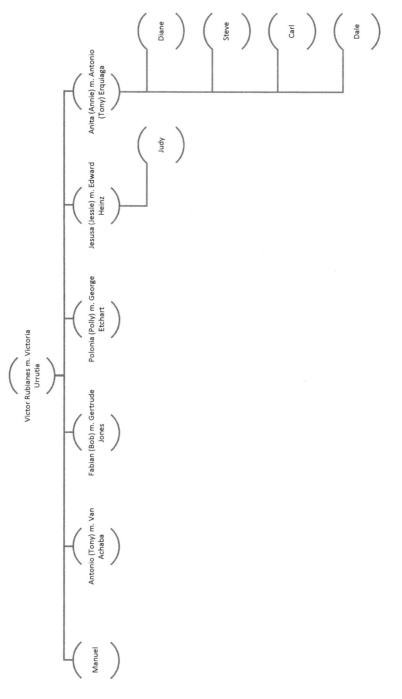

(Family tree of Marcelino and Eladia Erquiaga)

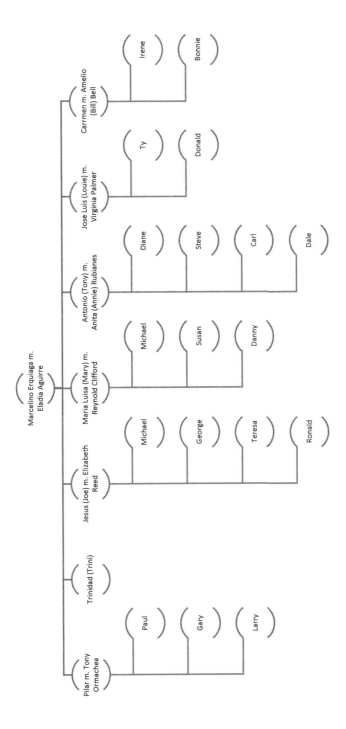

Paradise Valley

Winnemucca

Battle Mountain

Italian Grass
Canyon Valley

Reno Fallon Boyer Austin
Ranch Kingston

Ione

Las Vegas

N
W E
S

PROLOGUE

January 1, 1950
Fallon, Nevada

The wedding date was set for January 2, a Monday. It was to be a small, informal affair with only immediate family invited. The bride, with her family and friends, had spent considerable time reading Emily Post's *Etiquette* during the cold winter evenings leading up to the big day. For some reason, the men enjoyed reading about very formal weddings; all the "dos" and "don'ts" struck them as funny. The women dreamed big and planned small: something borrowed (a prayer book from the bride's best friend); something blue (a lace handkerchief crocheted by her sister); something old (a pocket watch from her mother). Her dress was to be a street-length white wool suit. Her brother would give her away, her father having died when she was young.

The rehearsal dinner was held at a relative's house on the Sunday before the wedding. The bride found herself looking around the room at the members of two Basque families, coming together in a single event carefully managed by the women as the men seemed to sit idly by. There in the corner was her mother, beaming with pride and happiness that even now, as a widow, she would see her last child married. Next to her, the mother-in-law-in-waiting, a woman the bride had yet to see smile even once, looked . . . not sad, but . . . absent. The bride thought about these two wives, seated now like queens on thrones, while around them the other women buzzed like a matrimonial hive.

The wives, she thought. *They seem to manage it all. And now I am to join their ranks.*

"Annie, we have a problem."

The bride's mother interrupted her musings.

"What now, Mom?"

"Count. Count the peoples. There are thirteen."

Without further explanation, the bride understood the problem. For her superstitious mother, thirteen people could not sit down for supper, lest one of them later die.

"Mom, you know that's just an old wives' tale," she tried to explain. "Yes, there were thirteen people at the Last Supper, but Jesus was supposed to die. That was the Lord's plan. It is not going to happen here."

But her mother would not hear of it. She refused to sit down to dinner if there were thirteen guests. The flustered young bride turned to her sister-in-law for help.

"Add another seat," the other woman said, and she headed out the door.

It was all the bride could do not to cry, but she followed instructions and set another place. In a loud voice, she called for everyone to sit at the two tables that had been artfully arranged, filling every available space in the cramped dining room. Her mother glared and remained standing in the kitchen.

The sister-in-law returned in short order, a neighbor woman in tow. There was a moment of confusion when the newcomer announced she had already eaten, but then it became clear she was happy to sit with the wedding party for coffee and dessert to "avoid any difficulties."

With that, the two families, including the bride's mother, took their places. The bride looked around the room again, eyeing the relatives for a few seconds as she thought of the many things that had transpired to bring them here from across the sea, through good times and bad. They all had stories worth telling. She felt someone should make a speech, celebrate what was happening. But no one seemed up for the task.

What the heck, she thought.

The bride stood and tapped her glass with the edge of her salad fork, just as she had seen men do when offering a toast at the political dinners that she sometimes had been lucky enough to attend through her job in the state's capital city. All the guests looked her way and smiled, some reaching for their glass as they realized what she was about to do.

"To the wives, me included!" she said, gesturing with her glass to the two matriarchs.

The bride's mother laughed and clapped. The mother-in-law wiped a tear from the corner of one eye.

"To the wives!" everyone cheered.

PART ONE:
Beginnings
1896–1916

VICTORIA
Amoroto, Spain
November 1896

Victoriana Urrutibeascoa sat alone by the fire in the main room of her parents' house, crying. The body of Antonio Urrutibeascoa de Urcadegui lay in his bed in the next room. The priest was still in there, with the girl's mother, Maria Carmen.

In one hand, Victoriana held her father's pocket watch. If she listened closely, she could hear the ticking sound that had always comforted her to sleep on cold nights like this. But, for once, there was no comfort in the sound because, somehow, she had caused her father's death. Victoriana was only eight, but she knew about evil spirits and bad luck. Her mother was always telling her what not to do, and what she must do, to move through the world safely. But she hadn't listened.

Antonio had caught his death of cold during a recent fishing voyage on the Bay of Biscay. Coming and going from the port of Lekeitio was commonplace; the young farmer and father of four often supplemented the family income and stocked the cellar by joining a fishing crew. While he was gone, his wife made sure their daughter and three sons minded their manners and did nothing to upset the ancient spirits of Basque tradition or the Holy Ghost that the village priest tried to explain to Victoriana whenever he had the chance.

Whistling was forbidden in the Urrutibeascoa house when Antonio was at sea.

"The ocean is quick enough to blow up a storm that can sink your father's boat," Maria Carmen told her children. "You don't need to add evil winds to the air with your whistling."

Antonio laughed at his wife's superstitions.

"I told you that fishermen don't like whistling on the ship, for fear of the storms," he would say, "but that doesn't mean the kids can't have a little music at home."

Maria Carmen had never accepted his explanations, and Victoriana knew it. Still, she liked to whistle and, whenever she was away from her mother and brothers, she did so.

That brought the storm. The storm nearly sank the boat. Her father caught the influenza from being wet and cold. And now he was dead in the next room. It was simple.

"Victoriana."

Her mother stood in the doorway, a candle in one hand.

"Come and say goodbye to your father. God has taken him to Heaven."

Victoriana rose from her chair, slipped her father's watch into the pocket in the waistband of her skirt, and went to face her judgment.

ELADIA
Donostia-San Sebastián, Spain
June 1900

The contessa stood with her charge at the entrance to the ballroom, her hand pressed firmly into the space between the little girl's boney shoulder blades.

"Hold your chin up high, Eladia, but keep your eyes down, looking at the floor. I will be right beside you as you walk. One, two, three . . . begin."

She smiled as the child, tall and thin for her age, with dark brown hair, took one hesitant step, then another, then another. Soon they were moving together into the spacious ballroom with its wall of windows facing the ocean. The contessa's hand dropped to her side. The child needed no further prodding.

From somewhere they heard violins playing, and there was a steady murmur of courtiers and others in the presence of Her Majesty Queen María Cristina, but as the contessa and Eladia moved through the room, they paid little attention to the background noise. Eladia was focused on somehow determining, without looking up, how far away the Queen was, and the contessa was too proud to care what other personages could be found in the royal presence on this day. She had brought her protégé to the summer court of Spain's royal family, which annually escaped the heat of Madrid by traveling to the cool northern Basque Coast, to present the young girl to Spanish society.

A man to their left coughed. The duo stopped.

Eladia looked up, briefly, just enough to see the Queen smiling down at her from a dais on which perched a rather ordinary chair not unlike those in her own home. She quickly returned her gaze to the floor as instructed.

"Your Majesty," the contessa began. She paused to clear her throat. "I am honored to present my goddaughter, Eladia Aguirre de

Arroyabe, of Nanclares de Gamboa, the daughter of my cousins and dearest friends, Nicanor and Francisca."

There was a long pause until Eladia remembered she was supposed to curtsy. She quickly performed the proper motion, and the Queen spoke.

"We are pleased to make your acquaintance, Eladia. What a pretty dress you have on today. I like blue as well. We thank you for gracing the Court with its beauty, and your own, of course."

Eladia, unsure what to do next, curtsied a second time.

A soft, gentle laugh escaped the Queen's lips.

"How many years have you, Eladia?"

"Eight." Barely a whisper.

The contessa coughed.

"Eight, *Your Majesty*," Eladia tried again, this time a bit louder.

"Eight is a very fine number," the Queen replied. "And you, my old friend Contessa María del Pilar, are you well?"

"Yes, Your Majesty. I am well. My husband spoils me with the things I most appreciate, and we are fortunate to have the benefit of living in a Spain you rule as regent until your son comes of age." The contessa inclined her head slightly but did not curtsy.

Gentle laughter again. "You always know the proper flattery, Pilar. You, too, are most welcome here."

With that, the Queen cleared her throat in much the same manner as the contessa had, and Eladia found herself steered by her mentor back through the room the way they had come. Once outside the ballroom doors, she relaxed just a bit.

"There," the contessa announced. "That is a life well begun. You must never forget your place in society, Eladia. You will spend your life in rooms like that one, mark my words. Now it is time for tea, I think. Let us return to our hotel, Ladi. Well done."

Eladia curtsied, now purely out of habit, not knowing what to say. The contessa responded with a loud laugh, much different from that of the Queen, more cynical and almost mean-spirited. Eladia winced, wondering what she had done wrong this time, hating the world into which she was being steered and longing for something else.

VICTORIA
Lekeitio, Spain
May 1907

The girl with the chestnut hair lay on top of the bedcovers, wondering what time it was. Today was not the day to oversleep.

In fact, Victoriana Urrutibeascoa de Uberuaga, aged 19, had never overslept a day in her life, and she was certainly not going to begin now. In just a few hours, she would continue the long journey that would culminate in a distant town with a name she could not pronounce, somewhere in the western United States. She had begun her journey of immigration the day before, leaving behind her tiny hilltop village of Amoroto, where her family had lived for more generations than Victoriana could count. With her belongings carefully packed in an old canvas satchel, given to her by the village priest, the young Basque girl had walked the eight kilometers down the hill from Amoroto to the seaside town of Lekeitio. There she met her friend, Mikele, who would make the journey to America with her. The two had first become friends at a school for seamstresses in their early teen years, and the skills they acquired there had earned them the money necessary for immigration. Mikele was just three years older than Victoriana, but she carried herself with an enviable assurance.

The girls had spent the evening before walking along the port in Lekeitio, admiring the ocean bay where, once each year in a festival dating back centuries, the young boys of the town would tie geese to a cable over the water and then hang from the birds' necks for as long as they could. Victoriana did not understand the ritual, but she had always found the festival a grand and exciting time. Almost any trip to Lekeitio, though, was grand and exciting to her. In Amoroto there were fewer than ten families, one church, a cemetery, and a bar. No one hung by the neck of a goose there. In fact, nothing exciting ever seemed to happen in her village.

The two girls had taken lodging in a ramshackle hotel over the Bar Erkiaga, an establishment owned by friends of Victoriana's mother. The room was tiny, but free. And it was only for one night— before the grand adventure began in earnest.

The girl with the chestnut hair could wait no longer. She poked Mikele, who had been snoring quietly for some hours, rousing her from slumber.

"Get up, get up, you lazy cow! I want to get to America."

Mikele mumbled something young ladies should not say in polite company, but she slowly arose from bed next to Victoriana and stood, stretching.

"The sun isn't even up yet, *Vitori*," she muttered with a yawn, resorting to the endearing form of her friend's name in the hope it might earn her another few minutes of sleep.

"It doesn't matter," Victoriana declared. "I want to get to the train station on time, and it's a long way to walk."

With that, she began digging in her satchel for the pocket watch she had carried since her father died. Sure enough, the watch told a time that made Victoriana sufficiently nervous.

"We're already late," she said. "Move along."

Victoriana knew the day's journey would not be easy. The girls would walk a bit further along the coast until they reached a town with a train station. From there, the train would carry them over the Pyrenees Mountains and through all of France. They would leave for America from Le Havre, aboard the ship SS *La Touraine*. That was all they knew. Neither had ever left Spain. Indeed, once the train passed into the next province, chugging its way from Vizcaya into Gipuzkoa, both girls exceeded their respective lifetimes of travel thus far.

"Tell me the story again," Mikele said as she gathered her belongings and tied back her shiny black hair with a piece of blue ribbon. "I want to hear about America."

Victoriana smiled and sighed dramatically.

"I have told you everything I know, a thousand times at least," she teased. But she began the story again . . . In America, so she had been told, no one was ever hungry. Oh, surely, not everyone was rich, but even the poor farmers had work and food. Land and houses were so plentiful that every child could inherit something—not like in Spain, where the King's law of primogeniture ensured that only the oldest son would inherit the family house, leaving the other children (children like Victoriana and Mikele) to either marry well, join the church, or otherwise fend for themselves. In America, they had no king and no war. Not since the war with Spain in the girls' youth—a war America had won, it must be remembered. Surely that was a sign Spain's time had passed and this was to be America's century. Who could help but want to live in a country so large and powerful that it had won the war?

"I don't want to hear about the war," Mikele whined. "I want to hear about the husbands we can find there." She pinched her cheeks and smoothed her clothes.

Victoriana sighed. "Very well, if that is all you care about."

"Of course it is all I care about!" Mikele said, a little too loudly for the early hour in a slumbering hotel. Seeing the look on Victoriana's face, she dropped to a whisper. "If I don't find a husband soon, the little bit of money I have saved will run out. It's the same for you, and you know it!"

Victoriana knew her friend was right. The small nest egg she had saved from her job as a seamstress, even when paired with some extra coins from her older brother, Domingo, would not last long. Once all her transportation costs were paid, she would arrive in New York City with sixty American dollars in her pocket. It was a huge sum for her, and ten dollars more than immigration laws required every disembarking passenger to possess, but she knew it was still a drop in the bucket in the wealthy nation across the Atlantic. Not for the first time, she wondered if she would be in this situation were her father still alive.

When Antonio Urrutibeascoa had died just over a decade ago, he left his widow with four children: Santiago, the eldest son who had since left for America; Domingo, who now managed their small farm; Victoriana; and 11-year-old Pedro. Five mouths to feed in a village with little to offer. Life had not been easy. Not like it would be in America.

"True, true, we are not rich," Victoriana admitted with a sigh. "Yet! Now gather up your things and let's get out of here." She pressed her father's pocket watch to her lips, kissed it, and returned the sacred relic to its hiding place in a zippered corner pouch of her satchel.

The girls emerged from their hotel room and sneaked down the back stairs, each toting a satchel in one hand. The bags were heavy, and Victoria almost wished she had a basket instead. She could carry that on her head. In this way, she and Mikele had learned to carry baskets of vegetables to market and bring back fish or other supplies on the return trip. It was good for their posture, Victoriana's mother always said.

A light rain began to fall as the young pair made their way through the winding streets to the main road up a hill and out of town. Victoriana and Mikele worried their skirts would soon be heavy from the rain, and the hems would no doubt be muddy. Victoriana was especially proud of the skirt she wore for the long journey. She liked to make her own clothes, and she had done so since enrolling in the school where she met Mikele. She had crafted the skirt herself using a pair of pants left from her father's wardrobe. She could not remember many things about her father, but she did have a memory of sitting on his lap during the long winters, enjoying the scratchy feel of his wool trousers against her hands, his pocket watch held to her ear so she could hear the ticking sound over the crackling roar of the fire.

The journey to the next village took four hours on foot. Along the way, the girls talked about America—of course—and Mikele steered the conversation toward future husbands whenever she could. When they reached the train station, they had two more hours to wait, according to the time schedule posted on the wall and their corresponding tickets. As it turned out, the train was late, leading Mikele to complain anew about having to get out of bed so early. Three hours passed before they were safely installed in the dirty, smoke-filled passenger car, headed into France. Victoriana did not mind; the journey would be worth it.

***

The port of Le Havre was bustling and, for two young girls who had barely left their home villages, it was a terror to behold. With some difficulty—no one here spoke the girls' native Basque, and neither girl spoke much Spanish and even less French—they found their way to the small café on a side street to which they had been directed by friends at home. Here they met up with Señora Lucia Cervantes, a matronly woman who made it her business to help young Spanish emigrants on their way to America.

"Welcome!" the Señora called, holding her arms wide as if she meant to embrace the two girls at once. "You have had a long journey, yes? Well, sit and have some hot soup, and then we will see you to the harbor and you will be on your way."

Señora Cervantes spoke Basque, Spanish, French, and, she said, a few words of German. It was her business to be so worldly, and Victoriana marveled at her talents.

The girls inhaled the soup noisily, not hesitating to ask for more, and then Señora Cervantes advised that they should visit the toilet and wash their faces.

"You will not enjoy the ship's accommodations, I am afraid," the Señora warned. "But the passage is not long—a few days only. Soon, you will be Americans!"

She said this with a tone of congratulations, but it was also clear that she shared no interest in herself becoming an American. Europe was fine by her, as she was soon explaining in detail how much money was to be made in helping the flood of emigrants leaving the European continent. Victoriana wondered if the emigrants all knew something Señora Cervantes did not, but she kept quiet.

Victoriana had no comprehension of what miracles Señora Cervantes had worked as they traversed the port city, but soon she found herself on the gangway waving goodbye to the older woman. Mikele began to cry, but Victoriana poked her in the ribs in a companionable way.

"Cheer up," she said. "Think of the future husbands in America!" With that, they smiled at each other, raced to the top of the gangway, and found their way to steerage class aboard the SS *La Touraine*, which was to be their home for the next eight days.

The journey proved to be remarkably uneventful. The two girls whiled away their hours playing games, singing songs, and walking on the rear deck when weather permitted. For one whole day, Mikele flirted with a French boy with long curly hair, but the language barrier prevented even that dalliance from adding much excitement to the trek. The ship plowed ahead through Atlantic waves. The girls slept more each day. Finally, exactly eight days after waving goodbye to Señora Cervantes, as dawn began to break, they reached their destination. The spires of New York City came into view, and the Statue of Liberty soon appeared.

Victoriana counted on her fingers quickly. The date was May 12, 1907.

"What time is it in America?" she asked. "I have to set my father's watch to this new world."

Mikele ignored her friend and leaned over the railing, waving at anyone and everyone who waited on the docks. Victoriana was too nervous to wave. She was worried about how they would make it through the immigration process, since neither of them spoke English.

After disembarking, the girls shuffled along, one line after another. It was in one such line, to their surprise, that they found a family of Basques. The wealthy Goicoecheas—a husband and wife with three children—were immigrating to live with relatives in Idaho. They had traveled in second class, with their own dining room and "deluxe" cabins quite apart from Victoriana, Mikele, and the many passengers squeezed together in steerage.

Mrs. Goicoechea professed to be most impressed that Victoriana and Mikele had made the journey alone without mishap.

"I would have been afraid to leave our home in Bilbao at your age," the woman announced. "You are so brave."

Mr. Goicoechea, who had been to America before, led the way and explained the various steps the girls would go through in their many hours of working their way through the immigration services at Ellis Island. His predictions all proved to be true, and soon Victoriana found herself at the head of what would be the last line, facing a grumpy woman with blonde hair who scowled at her paperwork and said something that sounded like her name, but which was accompanied by so many foreign sounds that Victoriana could make no reply. She smiled and nodded. The woman barked a few more words of what sounded like a question, gesturing at Mikele who had just passed through the woman's stall. Victoriana nodded again, smiling enthusiastically.

With a sigh, the blonde woman made some marks on Victoriana's papers, then wrote what the young girl would soon come to recognize as her somewhat shortened name on the outside of a folded sheet, stamped the lot with a giant mechanical device that made a loud and satisfactory clunking sound, and waved Victoriana through.

As she passed through the last set of doors into the open air, the girl with the chestnut hair looked at her papers for the first time. She was puzzled at first and then realized what had happened. The lady with the sad face had rewritten her name, shortening it from the original, albeit cumbersome, Victoriana Urrutibeascoa. There on the page before her, she saw the new yet familiar words: Victoria Urrutia.

She smiled at her new American name.

***

With the help of the Goicoechea clan, the girls made their way to the train station. They all traveled together as far as Salt Lake City and then the Goicoecheas changed trains for Boise while Victoria and Mikele continued to the tiny town of Winnemucca, Nevada. Victoria's brother Santiago Urrutibeascoa and his dour-faced wife, Aquilina, were waiting for them at the train station.

"We thought you would be here yesterday," Aquilina said with a sniff. "We had to come both days and there is no one else to watch the hotel while we are away."

Victoria had never met her sister-in-law, Santiago having married just two years ago here in Winnemucca, but she took an instant dislike to the older woman. How could she be held responsible for the schedule of ships and trains and government immigration workers? And who asked Aquilina to come greet them anyhow? Seeing Santiago would have been welcome enough.

"We came as soon as we could," was all she said aloud. "And now I will be here to work at the hotel. Mikele also."

Aquilina sniffed again. But Santiago laughed. "Welcome!" he said in a loud voice and hugged both girls, asking about the voyage and telling Mikele that she should call him "Santi" like his family did. Herded by Aquilina, the little group quickly walked away from the station toward the hotel Santi and Aquilina managed on a lease from another family of Basques. The small town boasted several hotels, including two that catered specifically to the immigrating Basque population. The one Santi managed, the Bush Hotel, was among the poorest in quality, with only a handful of rooms and a small bar but no restaurant. Still, it was close to the Southern Pacific Railroad station, and there was enough work for two maids eager to fulfill their dreams.

Aquilina showed the girls to their room. They would have to share a bed, and the room had no closet for their meager belongings. Victoria did not mind at all. She breathed in the crisp high desert air with relish and, retrieving her father's pocket watch from the satchel, she hung the treasure by its chain from one of the bedposts.

"Enough!" Aquilina declared. "Mikele, I need your help in the bar tonight and, Victoriana, there is laundry to take out for washing. I will show you where to go. Welcome to America, I suppose."

ELADIA
Santander, Spain
July 1907

When the Aguirre children arrived for their annual summer vacation, the noise resembled the sound of a circus rolling into town or, if the boys were in a fighting mood, perhaps the din surrounding the running of the bulls in Pamplona. For the Aguirre children's mother, Francisca, the noise inspired a headache and a desire to sit alone on the beach.

"Boys! Boys! Silence!"

Francisca was close to losing her temper, and her daughter, Eladia, recognized the signs. At 15, Eladia was the eldest of nine children and therefore expected to help her mother and the servants keep some control over the day's operation of unloading the family's small touring car plus two large horse-drawn wagons filled with people, steamer trunks, a spinet piano, and two large grey wolfhounds.

"Mama, why don't you go inside?" Eladia asked. "Concha can take little Eduardo, and Feliciana as well. Have her air out the parlor while I serve as shepherd to these boys."

Francisca let out a heavy sigh and thanked her daughter. She nodded at Concha, one of the maids, and marched ahead to the house. The maid took the two youngest children in hand and together the group swept up the stone staircase into the Aguirres' summer house. The building had been closed all year, and Eladia was correct: it would need airing out.

Eladia turned her attention back to the wagons where another maid, a chauffeur, and a footman were trying to unload.

"Please be careful with that piano!" she cried.

The small upright spinet was teetering on the back of one of the wagons. "Mauricio, Vicente, Rufino! Stop fighting and get control of those hounds! Isidora, Ricarda, Filomena! Get out of the wagon and help with these trunks. The servants cannot do everything!"

Eladia grumbled to herself as she watched one of the footmen grapple with an especially large trunk. Thank the Blessed Virgin the air was cooler here in Santander than it had been at home in Nanclares de Gamboa. Whenever Eladia inhaled, she could taste the salt on the air from the nearby seaside. If she could just gain control of her siblings, perhaps she could escape for a walk before dinner.

"Señorita Eladia, where do you want the piano?"

Eladia turned to look at her family chauffeur, Santiago. She smiled at the middle-aged man, whom she always found so helpful and kind.

"Papa will want to hear the music on the back patio, Santiago, so we had better put it in the main dining room. I don't think there's another room big enough with doors facing the back of the house." Eladia paused as she thought how ridiculous it must seem to the servants that the family had brought a piano on vacation, even a small one.

"I am sorry about the stairs, Santi," she said, and she patted the man's arm.

"It is nothing, Señorita Eladia, and it is the smallest piano Señor Aguirre could find," said the chauffeur with a smile. "Here! You boys! Come help Diego and me with this thing!"

Trust Santiago to make things work, Eladia thought.

Each year since Eladia had been 10, the Aguirre family had escaped the summer heat of their hometown for the oceanside city of Santander. Her father Nicanor was on good terms with the bankers and financiers who were based in the city, and its location on the Basque coast, significantly cooler than Spain's interior, made it an excellent getaway for his family. Last year, Nicanor had purchased the sprawling stone villa, intending to spend the month of August relaxing there. When his plans had changed at the last minute just this week, Nicanor had sent his wife and children ahead with the domestic staff to put the house in order. He would arrive in a week's time and the family hoped to spend their vacation reading, swimming, and—in the case of Eladia and her sister, Isidora—practicing the piano.

"My father seems to think my life must revolve around the study of music," Eladia called after Santiago as he moved to take charge of the heavy instrument's journey into the house. "Practice makes perfect, he says!"

Eladia smiled, but in her heart the story of the piano and her father's plans for her education irritated her. If she was to be allowed to continue her education, and she acknowledged this was exceedingly rare for young women, she wanted to study something useful, not music. But her parents had decided her course in life was to marry well, not fill her head with literature, philosophy, or—worse—business. In their view, studying music meant Eladia would have the necessary polish expected of a high society wife. She dreaded the entire prospect.

Out of the corner of her eye, Eladia caught a glimpse of one of the wolfhounds bounding out into the street.

"Filomena! Will you please watch the dogs! They are going to scare the horses!"

Putting her hands on her hips, she marched toward the wagons.

"Do I have to do everything myself?" she called to no one in particular, but despite her tone, she laughed at the chaos around her. *Papa was right to claim some meeting kept him in the city*, she thought. *Who would want to be witness to this?*

VICTORIA
Winnemucca, Nevada
August 1907

"You cannot marry a man you have known for less than a month, *Vitori*! You are insane. You have spent only a few hours truly alone with each other, and the rest of the time he stared at you while you wiped down tables in the bar!"

It had been a blisteringly hot summer, but the high summer temperature was no match for how hot Mikele was feeling as she scolded her friend Victoria.

"Mother of God, for the hundredth time, Mikele, I am not like you." Victoria sighed and crossed her arms. "I am not pretty. I'm all of five feet tall. I have the face of a boy. And crooked teeth as well. Victor may be my only chance."

"Crazy person!" shouted Mikele. "He is not your only chance. We have been here less than three months. We work in a hotel—men come and go every day. That is the nature of a hotel!"

Victoria's face broke into a smile. She shook her head slowly.

"Oh, Mikele, you are too sweet," she whispered. "I know this is a hotel. I cannot function here. I am not meant to live in an American city, even one the size of Winnemucca. I miss my tiny village and the farm. I think I will never learn English, and the people here are too strange. They laugh at me. Remember the black man?"

Mikele did indeed remember the large black man who had stayed at the Bush Hotel on the American holiday of the Fourth of July. She remembered well how Aquilina had decided that it was time for Victoria, after not quite two months working as a maid, to learn to collect rent, and how she chose to start her sister-in-law's new assignment with a black man who had arrived on the late train from California two days ago but had not yet paid for his room. She sent the young woman upstairs with a fifty-cent coin in her hand as an example of what payment was expected. Victoria was extremely nervous, having never seen a black person in Spain. She need not have worried. The man stared at her with a big smile until she pointed to the coin in her hand and muttered in her broken English, "Gimme dis." He laughed and handed over the fee, but Victoria was so embarrassed she had refused to interact with the customers ever since.

All of them except Victor Rubianes, that is.

Victor was 21, just two years older than Victoria, but had lived in America from the age of 13. He had immigrated with his parents, Manuel and Emeteria, his older brother Jenaro, and his two sisters, Polonia and Juanita. Back home, the Rubianes family had lived in Ea, a village just a few kilometers west of where Victoria had grown up.

Wanting her children to succeed in America, Emeteria had sent them all to school in Winnemucca for at least two years—longer for the girls, for whom Emeteria hoped to secure wealthy American husbands. Her mission had proven partially successful, as both Polonia and Juanita had married successful sheep men, older and far richer than the two girls could ever have dreamed of finding in Spain. True, both men were also Basque immigrants, not the rich Americans for whom Emeteria had wished, but this was to be forgiven.

Victor and Jenaro secured work as ranch hands, and that summer they were putting up hay on the Quinn River Ranch, a few miles outside Winnemucca. They and several other workers from the area had come to town for a few days just after the incident with the black hotel guest, and the young Victor met Victoria at the Bush Hotel's bar when she was perhaps most in need of being reminded of home. It was a relief to sit with someone who, although not family, spoke her language, and who knew all the places she knew back in Spain. Although she had never traveled to the village of Ea, she was familiar with the tiny hamlet of Arrigorri, where Victor said he had been born, and Ondarroa, where his sisters had been born.

Victor seemed safe to the shy young immigrant girl. She missed her mother more every day, and somehow, she liked the idea of having a man of her own—a man who would be around the house to replace the dead father she could barely remember from the winter fireplace.

And then there was the business of their names.

"Don't you think it's Fate speaking?" Victor asked with a wry smile. "Victor and Victoria, male and female, with the same roots. Shouldn't that mean something?"

At first Victoria could not tell if Victor was kidding, but over the few days that he and his friends were in town, he had made a point of crossing paths with her more and more. He tried to teach her a few words in English and laughed heartily when she told the story of the fifty-cent piece and the black man from California. Under Aquilina's watchful eye, they spent as much time together as they could. Victor had returned to the ranch for two weeks, only to return to Winnemucca, ask Victoria to dinner at the neighboring Martin Hotel, and propose marriage. She had accepted on the spot. That was three days ago, and Mikele had been badgering her every waking hour since, as much out of jealousy that Victoria had found a husband first, as from any concern for her friend's future well-being.

"Mikele, let me tell you one more time," Victoria said with newfound determination. "I am going to marry Victor when he comes back in a month. He went to find a ranch for us to lease, and I'm going to get out of this town, away from strangers and fifty-cent pieces and, I hope, the English language. I am happy to be a ranch hand's wife. That is final."

Mikele made a rude noise that involved her lips and tongue, which only caused Victoria to laugh. Soon her friend was laughing as well. It was hard to stay mad at a time like this.

A pounding sound came at the door to their room.

"We do not have time for girlish laughter," barked the voice of Aquilina. "If I am soon to have only one maid to do the work, more of it must be done now in preparation."

Mikele made the rude noise again, and the girls collapsed on their bed, holding their sides as they heard Aquilina's heavy footsteps trudge away.

The next month passed quickly. Mikele resigned herself to Victoria's impending marriage and began to examine the men of the town in earnest for herself. Somehow, the idea that Victoria, who was in fact quite plain, would find a husband first, had never occurred

to anyone. Nonetheless, Victor and Victoria were married upon his return to town, just as planned, on September 3, 1907. Standing before the justice of the peace, Victoria met her brother-in-law Jenaro Rubianes for the first time. He was joined by a friend of Victor's, and together the two men witnessed the marriage. With Mikele the only other person present, Aquilina having insisted that Santi stay at the hotel with her to work, the ceremony was soon over.

The young couple spent the night in the same upstairs room at the Bush Hotel where Victoria had asked the black man for his rent. Victor, who had more romantic experience than the sheltered Victoria, tried to make a joke by repeating the "Gimme dis" phrase in the throes of passion, but the young girl wanted nothing to do with his humor. As Victoria drifted off to sleep, she wondered for the first time if she were too serious for her carefree husband.

The newlyweds awoke in each other's arms the next morning, packed Victoria's satchel, said goodbye to friends and family, and climbed into a horse-drawn wagon Victor had procured with the Kane Springs Ranch. They began the trek to their new home in silence. Victoria clung to her father's pocket watch for the entire trip.

ELADIA
Nanclares de Gamboa, Spain
January 1912

The sisters strolled along the paseo at the Plaza Mayor. Arm in arm, they admired the shop windows as they passed. Although the holidays were over, the stores were still decorated for Three Kings Day, tantalizing passersby with sweets, candles, and bolts of lush wools and silks. In the street to the girls' left, about fifty feet behind them, a sleek black motorcar rolled slowly along, keeping pace. The car's sole occupant, a man behind the wheel, had a chauffeur's cap pulled down low on his forehead.

"Ladi, look!" squealed the girl closest to the store windows. "That material is beautiful! Look how it shines! It would make a lovely gown for the Governor's Ball!"

Eladia Aguirre laughed and allowed her younger sister to steer her to the window.

"Yes, yes, Isidora, I see it," she said. "And you are correct: it would make a lovely gown. But who says you are going to the ball?"

Isidora unlinked her arm from her older sister and struck a defiant pose, pointing with the index finger of one hand.

"Papa says!" she boasted. "I am 18 as of December, and so I am eligible."

Eladia smiled. "Oh, so ancient you are now! You had better find a husband soon or you will be an old maid." She playfully jostled her sister with one shoulder and then returned her gaze to the silk in the shop window. Eladia, aged 19, had no intention of attending another society affair with her parents, who had cut short her education out of fear of her already rebellious nature. She had briefly considered becoming a nun, but because she was the eldest child, her father had other plans. His business would benefit from a well-made marriage, and that meant she was often paraded at social functions.

"It is very pretty material," she mused aloud.

"Almost pretty enough for one such as you."

A man's voice interrupted the sisters' window-shopping and daydreaming. They turned to find a short man, perhaps a few years older than they, standing on the paseo a few feet away.

Eladia reached for her sister's hand.

"Pardon, sir," she said coldly. "We did not know we were being overheard. Please, do not let us interfere with your shopping."

The man laughed as he spoke again. "Oh, I am not shopping, lovely lady. I am selling. Singer sewing machines—the best in the world. They come from America." He paused for effect.

"Like me," he added with a grin.

"You are an American?" exclaimed Isidora. "You sound Spanish."

Eladia shushed her sister nervously but looked directly into the stranger's eyes. There was something about him she rather liked.

"I am Spanish," the man admitted. "But I have lived in America and have returned with my fortune to find a wife." He winked. "Marcelino Erquiaga de Ibarguren, at your service, ladies." He bowed low in greeting.

Eladia laughed. "Pleased to meet you, Señor Erquiaga." She did not volunteer their names.

Marcelino took a card from his coat pocket and offered it to Eladia. She stared down at it with a look of indifference, as if he had offered her a stone from the street. Isidora, however, giggled and grasped the card.

"I would be happy to call on you, if you would allow it," Marcelino said, still grinning.

Isidora nodded and blurted out an enthusiastic reply before Eladia could silence her.

"Our father is Nicanor Aguirre, the businessman. You can find his house on the Calle Echeverria, number six!" Isidora looked quite pleased with herself, but Eladia glared and quickly pushed her sister toward the store in an effort to escape.

"Tomorrow, then!" Marcelino called after them as the shop's door opened, the tinkling of the bell on its handle punctuating his words. He turned and looked at the motor car which was now parked near the storefront. He tried to make eye contact with its driver and tipped his hat before striding away, his head held high.

**

Eladia let out another laugh, her hands clasped to the sides of her face.

"Stop!" she pleaded. "You are just too much! You make my cheeks hurt from laughing."

Marcelino smiled and laughed along with the young woman, pinching one of his own cheeks as he did so.

"You enjoy my stories of life in America?" he asked.

Eladia nodded. "Oh, yes, ever so much," she said. "I still cannot believe half of them, though. Did you really work in the mines, underground, searching for gold?"

Marcelino sat up straight. "I did. And for the king's ransom of $3.25 per day!"

The young couple was seated in the drawing room of the Casa Aguirre. They remained a respectful distance from each other, coffee and cakes spread before them on an ornate wooden table. Eladia's younger brother, Rufino, played in one corner with toy soldiers. The housekeeper who admitted Marcelino when he called had insisted the boy remain in the room, since all the adults and older children of the house were away.

Marcelino had arrived carrying a large trunk emblazoned on one side with the name of the Singer Company and filled with merchandise, but his wares were soon abandoned as he regaled Eladia with tales of his American adventures. By the ebony clock resting on the white marble mantelpiece, Eladia could tell almost two hours had passed since Marcelino's arrival. She did not mind at all.

"When the gold ran out, I left the mines and herded sheep in the mountains. Nevada's climate is much drier than Spain, at least our part of Spain. There was little rain, so my sheep were always dusty. One day—"

The sound of a throat clearing interrupted Marcelino's tale.

Eladia, still smiling, turned toward the sound. Her father stood in the doorway to the parlor. As her smiled vanished, she leapt to her feet and dropped a small curtsy.

"Papa!" she said, a little too loudly for the size of the room. "You have returned."

The man in the doorway cleared his throat again before responding. "Yes, and apparently just in the nick of time." He looked toward Marcelino, who was still relaxing on the yellow upholstered chair.

Eladia cleared her own throat and raised her eyebrows as she met Marcelino's gaze, willing him to rise. He remained seated.

"Papa, allow me to present Señor Marcelino Erquiaga de Ibarguren," Eladia said. "Señor Erquiaga, this is my father, Señor Nicanor Aguirre y Martinez de Apellaniz." When Marcelino still did not stand, instead touching the index finger of one hand to his forehead as if tipping a hat, she nervously forged ahead with her introductions.

"Señor Erquiaga came to show me a sewing machine, Papa," she said. "Isn't that generous? Isidora and I thought we might make gowns for the Governor's Ball. Wouldn't that be wonderful?" She paused, looking back and forth between her stoic father and the still-smiling, but still-seated, Marcelino.

"That seems very . . . industrious," said Nicanor Aguirre as he half turned to walk away. "It was a pleasure to meet you, Señor Erquiaga. I think it is time for my daughter to study her piano. Go with God."

"Yes, sir, I will!" called Marcelino as the older man walked away, his footsteps echoing on the marble floor. "And I look forward to seeing you again!"

VICTORIA
Paradise Valley, Nevada
February 1912

Victoria felt the contraction take hold and tried to breathe through the pain as best she could. She gripped the hand of the midwife, her friend Catherine, and waited. The pain passed and she sat back in the bed to relax.

"What will you name the child?" asked Catherine.

Victoria smiled. "Victor and I cannot agree. It was easy with the first two—Manuel is named for Victor's father and Antonio is named for mine. Now we are out of boys' names, so I hope this one is a girl."

The midwife laughed, but Victoria's smile was replaced with a grimace as another contraction began.

"It is time," said Catherine. She began to pull away the bedsheets and quickly left to get the water that was heating on the kitchen stove.

Through the pain, Victoria thought about her two sons, now aged three and two. They were healthy and happy youngsters, and the family had a good life in Paradise Valley. She and Victor had not lasted long at the Kane Springs Ranch, Victor declaring he was not cut out to run the place alone. Within a year of their marriage, they found themselves in the verdant Paradise Valley township, where her brother, Santi, and his wife managed another hotel. Victor found work as a buckaroo, a profession he liked because its American name derived from the Spanish word for cowboy, *vaquero,* and because he could largely set his own hours out on the range. Victor's father, the elder Manuel, and brother, Jenaro, were frequent visitors. The thought of her in-laws made Victoria smile through her pain. If the baby were a girl, Victoria certainly would not be naming her after Victor's mother. Victoria was terrified of her mother-in-law, with her one blind eye and constant criticism. It had been a blessing when Emeteria and her daughters had returned to Spain a year ago.

Victoria's thoughts were interrupted by another contraction, and she soon found herself unable to concentrate on anything but the midwife's instructions. Mercifully, the birth was quick.

"It's a boy!" announced Catherine.

Victoria, trying to take deep breaths, was unsure what to do with this knowledge. What would they call another boy? Perhaps she would wait and ask Victor.

"Since you do not have a name, we should consult the Calendar of Saints," Catherine said.

The midwife walked back to the kitchen and returned with the calendar. Victoria's sister-in-law had brought it back from Winnemucca right after New Year's. Victoria knew the Catholic tradition well: babies were often named for the saint on whose designated day they happened to be born. Feeling like she was about to doze off, Victoria managed to get out a simple question.

"Who will it be?"

"Saint Fabian! What a fine name for such a strong son. I will tell his father the good news when he gets here."

This sounded fine. So did a nap. Victoria was soon asleep, leaving her friend to care for little Fabian.

ELADIA
Nanclares de Gamboa, Spain
February 1913

Eladia sat quietly in the parlor of her parents' house, her black mourning clothes a visual manifestation of her dark mood. She sat alone on a blue velvet sofa. Across from her in matching chairs set beside the fireplace were two of her sisters. Their mother sat at the piano in the corner of the parlor. All were attired in black.

"Mama, please stop sitting over there if you are not going to play any music," the young woman finally said, breaking the silence that seemed even deeper in the hot, stuffy room.

Her mother looked up.

"Eladia Aguirre, you know it is improper to play music when a house such as ours is in mourning. If you had your way, we would host a dance and pass around a jug of cheap wine while men from your father's warehouses played the fiddle and the accordion."

This short speech elicited giggles, quickly stifled, from Eladia's younger sisters, Isidora and Filomena, but Eladia only frowned more. Try as she might, she could muster only so much sympathy for her mother over the loss of her uncle—a man they had rarely seen because he had lived in faraway Sevilla, a long journey from the Aguirre home in the small town of Nanclares de Gamboa.

"Then you could dance with Marcelino, Ladi!" teased Isidora.

Her own joke sent Isidora into paroxysms of laughter, soon joined by Filomena. In reply, the scowls on Eladia's face and that of her mother looked made from the same mold.

Francisca Fernandes de Arroyabe y Errasti was at best a sullen woman. Her daughter's frivolous dalliance with the Singer sewing machine salesman, Marcelino Erquiaga, caused her brooding nature to spiral into outright anger. For her, there was nothing to laugh at.

The young man had come calling, as salesmen do, gaining admittance to the imposing Case de Aguirre, a two-story stone structure with a garden and high wall, clearly the grandest residence in the town. And because the housekeeper had the brain of a gnat, Francisca believed, Marcelino had been left all but alone with Eladia and somehow had swept the girl off her feet with his tales of having gold in his pocket and a dream in his heart of becoming a businessman. The couple had stolen time together for a year. Eladia was smitten. Francisca and her husband, Nicanor, were apoplectic. "Eladia, do you not have some lace handwork or embroidery to occupy your time?" Francisca offered, attempting to quiet her other daughters. "I thought the mantilla you wore to Uncle Pedro's funeral seemed tired. Surely you can find something nicer when we accept callers later this week."

Isidora poked Filomena in the side and whispered, "Maybe she can stitch something up on a Singer sewing machine!" More laughter from beside the fireplace, a deep sigh from Francisca, and a huffing sound from Eladia as she rose and walked briskly from the room toward the front hall staircase.

If her mother could be described as sullen, Eladia would at best be termed withdrawn and at times standoffish. She was not unhappy, at least not until her parents had forbidden her to see Marcelino, but she was always closed off. With so many siblings, Eladia had found it hard to find her place in the family, so she resorted to needlework and long walks in the garden, or visits to the wealthy women in her mothers and father's social circle. And, of course, there was the piano.

Marcelino was quite the opposite. He was more alive than anyone Eladia had ever met. His family had moved to Nanclares when he was only eight months old, and he had grown up quite poor. He was open in his admission that travel to America in 1906 had been a gamble of last resort to avoid the draft and war in Morocco. Because it was unlawful for young men to leave Spain before serving in the Army, he had escaped to the Land of Opportunity. Five years later he had returned with money—actual American gold—and a confidence Eladia admired. She saw in him both an escape from her father's matrimonial plots and an exciting life outside the somber stone villas of her childhood.

Marching away from the parlor, Eladia found herself turning out the front door of her family home. She continued walking to the carriage house just outside the estate's walls. There she found Santiago, her family's chauffeur, polishing the sleek black touring car that was her father's pride and joy.

"Santi, I would like to go for a ride," she announced. "I do not care where. You decide."

Without further conversation, she climbed into the backseat of the car, then, settling in, pulled at the sleeves of her dress and smoothed the pleats of its skirt. Santiago made no comment and asked no questions. He merely took his place at the front of the car and drove. He pointed the car south and before long they were passing through Arroyabe, a town just a few miles from Nanclares, named for her mother's family. When she realized where they were, Eladia allowed herself to smile.

"You knew where to go before I did," she said. "They live just off the Plaza Mayor."

Marcelino's older sister, Tomasa, lived in Arroyabe, with her young son, Felix, and her younger brother, Zacarias. Her husband had already immigrated to America, and Tomasa was biding her time before joining him. It was to her tiny flat that Santiago drove. He parked on the central plaza and Eladia indicated she would not take long. She knew what had to be done.

Tomasa greeted her at the door of the flat with a smile, which turned quickly to a look of concern when she saw the grim set to Eladia's jaw. Zacarias was in the kitchen bouncing Felix on his knee, so she whispered as she drew Eladia to the corner of what passed for a living room.

"What is the matter? You look like a storm cloud."

"Do you have paper and something to write with?" Eladia asked.

Tomasa nodded and retrieved the requested materials from a drawer in the kitchen. In short order, Eladia had written a note and handed it to the other woman.

"Please give that to your brother as soon as you can. I know he is traveling around the province trying to sell sewing machines, but this is important."

Tomasa nodded. "Zacarias can find him. He has a friend with a car."

Eladia looked toward the kitchen.

"Thank you—both of you," she said. "You are my family now."

"So, does this letter say what I suspect it says?"

For once, it was Eladia's turn to smile. "It may. I cannot go on like this with my father and mother. The Casa Aguirre is a sad, sad place. I am asking Marcelino to come take me away, this weekend if he can."

Tomasa embraced Eladia, crinkling the all-important letter as she did so.

"We will be sisters," she whispered in her friend's ear. "At last, I will have a sister!"

VICTORIA
Paradise Valley, Nevada
September 1916

"*Vitori*, school is good for young people. They need to learn proper English," Victor declared. "I studied in Winnemucca when my parents first brought us to America. Now it's time for Manuel and Antonio to do the same."

Victoria pulled a face. She and her husband had been arguing for days about how to handle their children's education. Nearly a decade after her arrival in America, Victoria still felt she could not trust life's twists and turns. She and Victor had five children and a comfortable rental house in the town of Paradise Valley. Summers were bountiful times, with plenty of itinerant ranch work for Victor. Winters were leaner, with no crops to put up, but Victor made some money by trapping. Victoria fussed over her brood of children and helped at the hotel, still managed by her brother and his wife.

Victoria agreed, after a fair share of arguing, that Manuel and Antonio, aged eight and seven, could finally start school. That left her at home with Fabian, Polonia, and the baby, Jesusa. She was content, especially on Sundays when her younger brother, Pedro, who insisted on being called by his Americanized name of Pete, would join the family for dinner. Pete had immigrated in 1913, bringing with him the news that their mother had died. He, like Victor, picked up ranch work where he could, but relished the solitary life of a sheepherder most of all.

Saving what few coins she could from Victor's paltry wages, Victoria stitched the family's clothing from flour sacks and cloth salvaged from the occasional item left behind by travelers at the hotel. She loved it when the Basque families in the area gathered at the hotel for dances, often organized by Uncle Santi and Aunt *Mortzilla*—Aunt Blood Sausage—as the children came to call their pudgy, dour-faced relation. "She has fat fingers like blood sausages,"

Fabian had explained when his mother first caught him using the nickname.

"Fabian, don't be rude!" Victoria said with sternness in her voice, but a smile on her face. "If it wasn't for your poor aunt's garden, we would never see a vegetable in this house."

Antonio laughed at this.

"It's okay, Mom. He steals all of *Mortzilla's*—I mean, Aquilina's—green onions, too!"

One day Victor reported that his father had given up on the sheep business, selling all his shares to his son-in-law, Juan. Juan and his wife, Polonia, had made regular trips back and forth to Spain, and that spring they took the family patriarch with them to be with his wife. Victor's brother Jenaro was left to fend for himself herding sheep in central Nevada.

"America was hard on my father," Victor said when he relayed the news. "We are lucky compared to him."

Victoria shushed her husband. "Don't tempt Fate," she said.

***

Just before Thanksgiving, Victor was working as a buckaroo on a cattle drive many miles from town, and Victoria had gone to the neighbors to milk their cow. She wanted milk to make rice pudding for the children; she often bartered for milk and other supplies by sewing clothes for other families. The children, left unattended, began "horsing around," as Victor always called it, and Antonio decided to see what would happen if he tossed a match in the wood box next to the stove. Victoria came running when she saw the flames.

The fire quickly consumed the entire house and virtually all the family's belongings. They had only the clothes on their backs and, thankfully, a coffee can containing Victoria's pocket watch and the little money she had saved. By the time Victor returned to Paradise Valley two days later, Victoria—with Aquilina's help—had seen to disciplining the children and moved the family into an even smaller house behind the hotel. Victoria had little to say to her husband, blaming him for tempting fate in the first place. Increasingly angry, she knew at some level that she was punishing Victor for their economic circumstances, as much as her view of how bad luck might have caused their house to burn. She frequently wondered if Victor would ever find sufficient employment to provide for such a large family.

The situation did not improve as the winter snows arrived, and Victor was put out of work once more. He spent much of his time at the hotel bar, playing *mus*, a card game imported from the Old Country. The couple rarely spoke. Money was running out and so was Victoria's patience when one night Victor did not come home for dinner.

Perturbed by yet another of her husband's absences, Victoria fed the children and put the baby to bed. She checked her father's pocket watch for perhaps the tenth time since Victor had not appeared at the expected hour, and she reached for her hat.

"I am going over to the hotel," she announced. "Manuel, watch the children."

The short walk did little to calm Victoria's temper. The money from the coffee can was long gone. Victor's carefree, seemingly day-to-day approach to paid labor was no longer sufficient; Victoria wanted him to find a more permanent job. She had heard the hotel guests say that with war raging in Europe, jobs should be on the rise here at home, at least in the towns and cities. She did not want to leave the comfort of Paradise Valley, yet somehow she blamed her husband for not having a better plan.

As she entered the hotel bar, her anger was about to boil over. There at a table in the back sat Victor, apparently drunk, with a rich man from Battle Mountain, Juan Saval, for whom Pete had long worked.

"*Vitori!*" called Victor. "Over here!" He was clearly glad to see her, but she bristled at the familiar form of her name. Stiffly, she marched to the table. Victor stood as she approached, threw his arm around her waist, and whispered "Gimme dis" in her ear as he gently patted her fanny. Embarrassed and even angrier, she pushed him back into his chair and stood over the two men, her hands on her hips.

"Well?" It was all she could muster.

"*Vitori*, Mr. Saval here has purchased the Grass Valley Ranch from some wealthy banker," Victor announced. "Imagine! An immigrant so rich he can swindle an American banker out of good land! And I am to run it for him."

Juan Saval cleared his throat.

Victor smiled and shrugged. "Well, I am to help him run it. I am to be the head ranch hand. I will move to Grass Valley in the morning."

Victoria was unsure how to react. Here she had been frustrated that her husband had no plan when he suddenly presented her with one.

She hesitated just a moment before stiffening her back and her resolve.

"And what is to become of me and the children? Will you abandon the six of us here while you go off to this Grass Valley? I do not even know where that place is!"

Victor laughed.

"Oh, *Vitori*," said the young husband. "Grass Valley is not far from here, maybe two days' ride, out in the middle of Nevada by Austin. You and the children will move to Italian Canyon, much closer to Grass Valley, where Mr. Saval has provided us a with a fine stone cabin for our growing family. But do not worry! I will see you on the weekends."

Again, Saval cleared his throat.

"Victor, the cabin is small," Saval said. "How many children did you say you have?"

Victoria answered for her husband. "He has five children. And an angry wife. But we will not get in the way of your big American business deals, sir."

PART TWO:
A Rough Patch
1917–1918

ELADIA
October 1917
Vitoria-Gasteiz, Spain

"Children, children, we are going!"

Eladia fussed over her children like a hen over its chicks. Try as she might, she could not get the two girls and their brother to settle down and allow her to be sure they were ready for the afternoon's important visit.

"Children! The contessa is waiting. We are going! But first you must behave. I need you to sit down so I can comb your hair and be sure you are as clean as a shiny new coin . . ."

The sound of laughter and a light knocking interrupted Eladia's exhortations.

"When have the Erquiaga children ever seen a shiny new coin, let alone been as clean as one?"

Filomena Aguirre, Eladia's younger sister, breezed through the open door of the second-story flat, her face beaming and her arms open wide to hug the two squealing nieces who threw themselves into her embrace. "Good day, my sweet ones!"

"No need to be insulting, Filo," Eladia said with a sigh. "I thought you came to help me with the children, not to bring our father's message of doom and gloom into this house."

"Sister, please do not growl at me," the young woman said, conciliatory. "It is a happy day, and the sun is shining brightly. Of course, I am here to help you."

"Then see that you do," Eladia said as she reached out to snatch her son, Jesus, who careened by her at top speed, barking like a dog as he ran. Eladia made short work of smoothing Jesus' hair and straightening his errant shirt collar. She picked him up and set him none too gently on a rickety wooden chair by the door. "You sit," she ordered. Jesus scowled but did not move.

"Filo, get Pilar's comb from the bedroom while I try to make some sense of this lace Trinidad has all but ruined."

As Filomena took her niece by the hand and led Pilar to the single bedroom all the Erquiagas shared, Eladia tugged at her other daughter's hair and tried to untangle the lace shawl that Trinidad had tied around her waist.

"Trinidad, what have you done to this thing?" Eladia muttered. "The contessa is a very fancy lady. She will not be pleased with you. Is that what you want?"

Trinidad shook her head "no" and promptly put her right thumb in her mouth for comfort.

"Jesus, Trinidad—and if you can hear me, you too, Pilar—I am only going to say this one more time," Eladia said. "The contessa is an old friend of my family, and I have not seen her since Papa and I were married and came to live here in this apartment. Today is an important day. We have been invited to tea, and that is a sign of good fortune. Do you understand? Can you be good today?"

Trinidad nodded and the tiny Jesus plopped to the floor. Both were now sucking their thumbs. Eladia regarded her two children with a sense of foreboding. A great deal was riding on today's visit. She hoped the contessa would be pleased enough to help find a place in society for her children, as she had once done for Eladia herself.

"I understand, Mama!" came Pilar's voice from the other room. "Auntie has made my hair very nice, and I will be the best child of your family today!"

Eladia sighed and mumbled to herself, "That will be a first."

"I heard that, Eladia, and if I can hear you, the children can, too, so mind your whispers."

Filomena emerged from the tiny bedroom, leading a smiling, primping Pilar by one hand. "We are quite ready to go, and the children will be fine. The contessa is a lovely lady, filled with kindness."

"Ay, my God in Heaven, are you always this cheerful?" Eladia rolled her eyes. "Well, never mind, let's go. Filo, did you bring the car as I asked?"

Filo clicked her tongue. "Yes, of course I did. Papa thinks I am going into the Old City to shop, and Santiago is sworn to secrecy."

Eladia smiled for the first time that day. "Oh, Santiago! It will be so good to see him." She quickly scowled again, her face returning to what seemed its natural state. "But can we trust him not to tell Papa?"

"What can't we tell Papa?" asked Pilar, a tad too loudly.

"Shush. I am speaking of my father, not yours," Eladia said dismissively. "Mind your tongue and sit quietly until spoken to by an adult. We are going!"

In short order the two Aguirre sisters and all the children were out the front door, which Eladia carefully locked behind her, and making their way down the stairs to the street below where the Aguirre family chauffeur, Santiago, waited with a long black car.

"A car!" Pilar exclaimed. "Are we riding in the car?"

Eladia glared at her oldest child, and then turned to Santiago with another rare smile.

"Good day, Santi. I have missed you."

"Oh, Señorita—that is, Señora—I have missed you, too. The big house is not the same without you."

Filomena made a sniffing noise. "Yes, yes, the big house is not the same without her. Neither is the beach house. Or the flat in Madrid. All houses are different without Eladia, the scandalous one. Let's get moving." She helped the children into the backseat and gestured to her sister to ride up front with Santiago.

"No room for you back here," Filomena said bluntly.

Eladia ignored the intended slight and slipped her arm through Santiago's as he escorted her around the front of the vehicle and graciously opened the car door for her to sit. "You must tell me all the gossip, Santi," she said. "How are the servants? Are my siblings treating you well? What about Mama and Papa?"

Santiago merely smiled as he returned to his place behind the wheel. Eladia knew better than to ask a servant about his employers, so he suspected she was only teasing him as a way to distract from her sister's scolding. He nodded and declared all was well at Casa Aguirre. He started the engine and steered the car toward the hills outside Vitoria-Gasteiz. No one spoke for a time.

"Why does my grandfather hate my father, Aunt Filo?" Pilar asked, breaking the silence.

Eladia gasped. "Shush, Pilar! Such impertinence! I told you to be on your best behavior today and leave your auntie alone."

Filomena cleared her throat. "Never mind, Pilar. You do not need to worry about adult matters. We are going to have a lovely day. Tell me about the tavern your father and mother have. What is it like to live above such an exciting place?"

Eladia turned to glare at her sister, but she could tell Filomena had meant no insult. Her sister and the two girls were now chatting in conspiratorial whispers about what a fun life they had, how lucky they were. Little Jesus smiled but offered no commentary. He was clearly just enjoying the car ride. It was the first time the Erquiaga children had ridden in a private vehicle. Much different than the public bus they took around Vitoria-Gasteiz and, once, to the mountain village of Mondragon to visit their father's family. Eladia drew in a deep breath, exhaled slowly, and asked Santiago about his own family, a more suitable topic. Everyone seemed to relax and enjoy the ride to the contessa's home.

The house with the name El Jardín stood on a hilltop overlooking the Aguirre's ancestral hometown of Nanclares. It was the provenance of the Contessa María del Pilar Fernandes de Arroyabe y Errasti, a distant relative of Eladia's own mother, Francisca. The contessa's husband had been dead for five years, but the grand old dame ruled supreme in this region's social circle. There had been a time when Eladia, like all the Aguirre children, came and went from this house for social events and family gatherings. That had all ended when Eladia married Marcelino Erquiaga. Her contact with the family and her parents' friends had been summarily severed by her father, who was furious at her marriage to the pauper who had stolen the young girl's heart. Access to the Aguirre fortune was cut off as well.

Eladia sighed as she looked out the windshield of the car. A single tear pooled in the corner of one eye.

"We're here!" Pilar exclaimed as the car came to a stop in front of the grand house atop its verdant hill.

Eladia shook herself and took another deep breath.

"Children, remember your manners, and do not speak unless you are spoken to. This is a very formal household, and the contessa is an aristocrat."

"What is an aristocrat?" asked Pilar.

Filo snickered. "Heaven help us all," she said to no one in particular. Then, to Pilar: "It's a rich person who lives in a castle." She took Jesus by the hand as one and all disembarked from the sleek automobile. Santiago took up his post, standing formally by the rear of the car as his charges were escorted by the doorman who awaited them at the villa's entrance.

"The contessa is, of course, expecting you," the doorman announced, and he led the nervous little group beneath a tall iron archway and onto the grounds of El Jardín.

The garden for which the residence had been named certainly warranted the respect its title carried. Lush rose bushes mingled with fan palms, potted geranium plants, and countless shrubs drooping with heavy blossoms in every color of the rainbow. Here and there, the eye could spy benches and white marble statues of every size and shape. A fountain twice the size of the Aguirre's grand automobile blocked the central pathway, causing the doorman to navigate around it on a cobblestone walk that took the group beneath the drooping branches of a willow tree.

"It is beautiful, Mama."

"Yes, Pilar, it is beautiful." Eladia placed one finger in front of her lips and nodded at her child in warning. Soon they reached the doorway where two iron doors more than fifteen feet high were standing open, revealing the cool marbled interior of El Jardín itself.

"The contessa is waiting in the front parlor, to your left." With that, the doorman was gone, returning to the outside world on some unknown errand and leaving Eladia and Filomena to navigate their way the short distance to the brightly lit room off the foyer. The children tiptoed after them like baby ducklings walking through a puddle. Inside, the white and blue velvet upholstery of the furniture, each piece resplendent with more pillows than the one next to it, greeted them like a friendly embrace.

"Ladi, Filo, you are welcome in my home!"

The strong, almost mannish voice came from a tiny woman perched on a white velvet wing-backed chair drawn up next to a grand piano in one corner of the room. The woman rose as the two Aguirre sisters curtsied a greeting.

"Tut, tut, no formalities here, we are family!" the contessa assured. "Let me see the children. Which is my namesake? You, the taller one, are you Pilar?"

Pilar glanced nervously at her mother and then her aunt. Filomena nodded with encouragement.

"Yes, Señora, I am Pilar."

The contessa laughed, the tinkling sound of ice falling into a glass, quite distinct from her otherwise forceful voice. "Indeed, you are. And so, you must be Trinidad and you, Jesus." She did not extend her arms to touch any of the children. She merely appraised them, and then looked at their mother in a long, cold silence.

Without a glance at Filomena, she began issuing orders. "Filo, my dear child, take the children to the kitchen where there is a light refreshment waiting for the young ones, more to their taste. You may return in half an hour."

Filo's jaw dropped a bit, but the contessa had already turned her back and was seating herself once more on the wing-backed chair. She was dressed from head to toe in black lace and satin. She settled the folds around her primly as Eladia mouthed a silent apology to her sister and took a seat on the tiny sofa nearest the contessa's throne-like station. Filo, sensing defeat, signaled for the three children to follow. They exited the parlor just as Jesus started to cry.

"You see, Ladi, this way it will be so much easier for us to catch up. Children are a distraction. It is precisely why I never had any myself."

The contessa reached for a bell resting on a small table to one side of her chair and imperiously rang the little device. Eladia knew this was the sign for some unseen servant to bring tea or perhaps coffee with milk. She settled back on the sofa and waited for the verbal onslaught to begin. The contessa did not disappoint.

"You seem healthy, after your loss," the old woman began.

Eladia bristled for a moment, but exhaustion quickly took the upper hand. Leave it to this woman to remind her of the infant, dead less than a month, she had recently lost. Before Eladia could become too distracted by that grief, the woman in black continued.

"I will not ask you how your parents are, the poor dears, because of course I know you would have no knowledge of their well-being since you have so little contact. So instead, I will tell you the news. Nicanor is quite well, but your poor mother seemed weak the last time I saw her. No doubt this horrible influenza that has the country by the throat. All of Europe, I suppose, and even America. I do hope Francisca will not fall too ill. Are your friends in America suffering?"

Eladia took a deep breath. "Contessa, our *family* is quite fine. My husband's brothers and sister live in a place called Nevada."

"How droll—a Spanish name in that English-speaking country," the contessa said curtly. "Do you teach the children English? Or perhaps Basque, like your husband's family no doubt speaks in its quaint mountain farmhouses?"

Eladia grimaced. "We speak Spanish," she said after a pause. "And Marcelino's family is no more Basque nor less Spanish than you and I are, Madame."

The contessa sniffed. "Yes, but there are Basques and then there are *Basques*. Our family and friends have been a part of Greater Spain for generations. We do not cower in mountain villages. Why, your father was at court just last month, delivering some sort of goods to His Majesty himself. I do not pretend to understand the world of commerce in which your father operates, but I know the King appreciates the coming and going of all these manufactured items with the rest of the world at war. All of Spain marvels at the ability of your father's company to transport the goods we need. It is a blessing."

Eladia said nothing. The contessa forged ahead in the ensuing silence.

"And they tell me you run a tavern. You live above this tavern where you and your husband work. No more cameras to sell for him?"

"Sewing machines, Madame. He sold sewing machines, not cameras, but now he is a man of the restaurant trade—commerce, not unlike my father." Eladia was at last taking the bait and sitting up a bit taller, her voice laced with false amusement as she responded.

The contessa laughed the tinkling laugh once more. "Yes, Nico and this husband of yours must have so much in common. I am certain it would make lovely dinner conversation, if your father ever allowed the little Basque man who has been to America into any of his homes . . . Ah, the tea has arrived!" A maid in a starched gray dress appeared with a tray. "Just put it there. Eladia will pour. You may go."

The maid curtsied and fled as Eladia reached for the teapot and a tiny cup and saucer. "Milk?" she asked.

"Absolutely not. Thank you."

Eladia handed the cup and saucer to the grand dame and then poured one for herself, adding milk for spite, and sugar as well. She settled back on the sofa.

The contessa sighed and began again.

"I suppose you should tell me the story. It has been almost five years since you stepped foot in my house. I want to know your side of what happened."

Eladia cleared her throat and investigated her teacup. Should she tell this woman that she had made a mistake, made a bad marriage? That she had been pregnant for four years running, giving birth to child after child? That she was tired of working in a tavern they could barely keep afloat, tired of living over a bar with a husband who already had drunk too much even before they lived 20 feet from a liquor cabinet? That she missed her family and, most of all, their money? Should she just tell the contessa she was tired to her bones?

She looked up and realized the contessa was waiting for her to speak.

"Everything is wonderful," Eladia announced. She cleared her throat and leaned forward to place her teacup and its saucer on the tray, then folded her hands in her lap and began her story, or at least the edited version.

"Marcelino is a kind man, Contessa. True, he comes from a working-class family in the villages, and he will inherit nothing. But he is industrious and hard-working. He went to America when he was only 20 in search of work. He hiked over the Pyrenees to make his way to France and then to England, where he found passage to America."

Eladia paused. She did not mention that Marcelino had stowed away on a coal ship to reach Liverpool, England, and was barely able to afford the price of a steerage class journey from there to America.

"He arrived with nothing and worked for five years in that faraway place so that he returned to Spain with a great deal of gold, actual gold, in his pocket. It is true that he sold sewing machines in Vitoria-Gasteiz when he came back here, but now we run a respectable tavern. We have three children. The Lord took the fourth from us when she was but a few days old, an angel in the making, but those who remain are healthy and happy and polite. If you would only spend a little time with them, you would see."

The contessa laughed, this time a snorting noise instead of a tinkle. "I have seen. Their clothes are worn, and they have empty eyes. I am insulted that one is named after me. You surely did me no favor there."

"I meant to honor you. She is a bright child, intelligent—"

"Do not lecture me, girl. I am not feeling well today. I am feverish and my chest hurts. It has been a great stress for me to see you and witness this life you have made for yourself." She paused.

"I cannot help you."

"I did not ask for help, Contessa. We came because Filo said you wished to see the children. I want nothing from you."

Eladia began to get up.

"Sit down!" The contessa was clearly agitated now. Her breath became labored as she spoke.

"Your father was right to cut you off without a cent. Your siblings will need all the money they have. They will have many challenges. The King has lost much of his power due to the present war, Europe is ravaged, and now this influenza. You know they call it the Spanish flu? Such an insult. It comes from swine they say, and then they call it the Spanish flu!"

"I do not see what that has to do with me," Eladia said stiffly.

"It has everything to do with you. Life is changing, child. Most of the great monarchies will be swept aside once this so-called Great War is over. Look at what happened to the Czar! They say he has abdicated, and his family is being held hostage—imagine! What if this happens here in Spain? Your family's position is at risk. And you are living like a pauper over a tavern. With those children! What life is that for a child named María del Pilar, or any other brat you and that husband of yours have brought into this world. Have you nothing to say for yourself?"

Eladia cleared her throat. Then she cleared it a second time, stalling for time while she collected her thoughts.

"Yes, Contessa, I have something to say. Goodbye. Go with God."

Eladia stood and walked briskly from the room, out the front door, and to her father's waiting car. She shook her head at Santiago as he moved toward her, opened her own car door, climbed inside, and slammed the door behind her. Santiago hastened into the house and somehow found his way to the kitchen where he retrieved the rest of the clan. As they were leaving the house amidst whispers from the children and shushing sounds from Filomena, the sound of a deep-throated coughing fit came from the front parlor.

"What did you do to her?" Filomena asked as the car began its descent from the grounds of El Jardín. "She's in there coughing up a lung!"

"Good," Eladia said in a quiet stony voice. "I hope the old Spanish sow has the swine flu. It would serve her right."

"What is swine flu, Mama?" asked Pilar.

"Shush, child, not now," said Filomena.

Eladia began to cry. Realizing how poorly the important visit had gone, she suddenly recalled her long-ago visit to the Queen, described by the contessa at the time as "a life well begun." *So much for new beginnings*, she thought.

***

The priest stood in the upstairs hallway outside the tiny flat over the Erquiagas' *taverna*, his Bible in one hand and a bulky brass crucifix in the other. His hat was on his balding head. He was leaving.

"Marcelino, there is nothing more to be done for them," said the priest. "I have afforded them the sacrament of Last Rites. It is up to God now, whether they will live or die. If they die, they go with God. You must know this."

Marcelino did not make any sign of agreement or disagreement. He kept looking over his shoulder toward the bedroom where his wife and son lay confined to the same bed. They had been there for over a week.

"Thank you, Father. If you don't mind, I will seek help other than God's."

The priest arched his back and muttered something under his breath that Marcelino could not hear and did not care to hear. With that, the priest turned and walked down the stairs. Marcelino went inside the flat and closed the door softly.

"Filomena, I have to find someone to help. I cannot lose them both."

Filomena sat off to one side of the large room that housed the sparse dining and living room furniture. She had tried to make herself invisible during the priest's unfortunate visit.

"Tell me how I can help," she said now, standing and moving to Marcelino's side.

"Stay with them. I am going to go visit the girls and then . . . I don't know." Marcelino reached for his hat.

Pilar and Trinidad had been at a friend's house for several days, since Jesus fell ill with the same fever that had gripped his mother a few days after the visit to El Jardín.

"Of course, of course," Filomena said. "Give the girls my love. Now go."

Marcelino nodded and left the same way the priest had gone. When he reached the street, however, he did not turn left toward the friend's house but instead veered right and walked toward the Old City at the heart of Vitoria-Gasteiz. He wandered aimlessly for several minutes, fighting the incessant tug that drew him toward the doorway of every bar he passed.

Finally, in a section of the Old City he rarely visited, he succumbed. He entered a dark, seedy bar that smelled of rancid sausages and took a stool in the corner at the end of the counter.

"Brandy," he said to the bartender.

Three glasses later, he had forgotten the priest's grim visit. Yet another glass and he was talking loudly about how an aristocrat had infected his wife and only son with the influenza and wondering if the aristocracy carried a different kind of germ than the common folk. An old man sitting at the other end of the counter listened intently to Marcelino's ramblings. After watching the young Basque drink two more glasses of brandy, the old man walked over and clapped Marcelino on his back.

"I know someone who can help you," he said.

The sun was setting by the time the two men had conversed, paid their bar tabs, and made the journey from the bar to a wagon by the river on the outskirts of town. There Marcelino handed over what amounted to a great deal of money for one so poor, as well as the address of the tavern where the Gypsy traveler could come the next day to collect the remainder of his fee. In exchange, Marcelino left with a jar of foul-smelling tonic and instructions to cover every bit of his wife's and son's bodies with the stuff.

"Leave no small patch of skin uncovered, or they will surely die," the Gypsy warned. Marcelino nodded, still groggy from the brandy, and found his way home.

"Filo, you must go away now," he said as he stumbled into the flat.

The two argued for a time but Filomena finally acquiesced and, crying, took her leave. Marcelino locked the door behind her. He went about the business of stripping Eladia and Jesus naked, slathering their feverish bodies with the tonic, and trying not to vomit from the stench of the stuff. Then he passed out on the floor beside the bed the two patients shared.

Dawn came and still the trio slept. At about nine o'clock, Filomena returned with her younger brother, Eduardo. They banged on the door until Marcelino finally roused himself and let them in.

"You look awful!" little Eduardo exclaimed.

"What have you done?" Filomena asked, almost in the same breath with her brother's declaration.

Marcelino only shook his head and shuffled to the kitchen to pour a glass of water from the pitcher that sat in the windowsill.

"Mama?"

The small sound of Jesus' voice went through the flat like a shot. When Eladia's voice replied weakly, "Yes, my little son, I am here," the other three occupants of the flat scrambled to be the first to reach the bedroom.

"What is all the fuss about?" asked Eladia as the three stood by the bed staring. "And may I have a glass of water, please?"

VICTORIA
May 1918
Near Austin, Nevada

Victoria stood by the front door of the house in Italian Canyon, her eyes fixed on the road leading to where she was standing. Her brother, Pete, was due any minute. She had sent the children off to play, and Victor was away working at the Grass Valley Ranch, so she was looking forward to some time alone with her brother.

She had been forced to admit that the move from Paradise Valley was a wise financial decision. For over a year, Victor had enjoyed steady employment. The ranch was large, with cattle to be fed throughout the winter, so the work did not dissipate with the arrival of autumn. The ranch's assets included a roaming band of sheep, which Victor had arranged to have entrusted to Pete's care. Juan Saval made good on his word, and the men had prospered, even as America plunged headlong into the war in Europe.

The living arrangements were less desirable than Paradise Valley. The "small" cabin was in fact a single room, albeit one made of stone. It was cool in the summer and snug and warm in the winter, thanks to the wood-burning pot-bellied stove that stood in one corner. Since the house was stone, she reckoned her children might have more difficulty burning it down, at least. But five children, one barely 18 months old, under this tiny roof was a growing challenge, as were the resident rodents. The rats seemed to Victoria as big as cats; some would sit on the bedposts at night, watching their human housemates. Victoria kept a lamp lit near the baby's crib, so she could see the vermin. *At least there are no neighbors to hear me yelling,* she sometimes thought.There was no more school for the children, which even Victoria had begun to worry about. Victor came home every other weekend. Pete came whenever he and the band of sheep made their way to the high mountain pastures nearby, often bringing news of family and friends.

As Victoria watched Pete approach on horseback, she wondered if he had anything of interest to share. The siblings hugged and exchanged quick greetings. Pete carried two chairs into what passed as a yard on the east side of the house. He wasted no time before announcing that Santiago and Aquilina had at long last returned to Spain. Victoria took the news hard.

"We are the only ones left," she said, more to herself than to her brother.

"Oh, stop your complaining," Pete suggested. "Victor is doing the best he can, and I love it here. There is nothing for us in Amoroto, remember? Santi has the house now that Mama is gone, and because he has no children, the place will pass to Domingo, who stayed there all these years. Wouldn't you rather be living out on the land the way we are?"

Suddenly remembering her life as a hotel maid and the chuckling of the black guest, Victoria decided that she was indeed happier in the little stone cabin than she perhaps believed on the bad days.

"Tell me the news," she said with a smile, drawing her chair closer to Pete's.

Pete quickly turned somber.

"Of course, the news in town, at all the ranches, and from Spain itself is about the influenza," Pete said quietly. "They call it the 'swine flu' or 'Spanish flu' and say it has something to do with the Great War."

Victoria shook her head and made the sign of the cross. She, too, had heard of the plague ravaging Europe and showing itself on American military bases. Pete and Victor, neither of them yet American citizens, had avoided President Wilson's experiment with world warfare. Life was hard enough on the ranches of central Nevada without thought of the battlefields of Europe. But the influenza acted in even more frightening ways than the American government and its new military machine.

"Do you know anyone who has been sick?" Victoria asked cautiously.

Pete shook his head. "Not yet, but they say everyone will know somebody before this is over."

***

The sound of coughing woke Victoria from a deep slumber.

She lay in bed for a few moments, trying to discern which of her children was coughing and whether there was any seriousness to the situation. Within seconds, the sound of retching convinced her something was wrong. This sound clearly came from the bed Polonia and Jesusa shared, over by the stove.

"Mother is coming, little ones," she called, and within seconds she was standing by the bed her daughters shared. The coverlet was wet with vomit. Polonia was awake.

"Here, sit up. Let me clean you off. What's wrong?"

"Sick," was all the child offered. Before she could continue, the coughing sound returned, and Victoria now realized it came from Manuel's bed.

"*Manolo*, are you sick?" she called.

More coughing and then silence.

Victoria reached for the kerosene lantern kept atop the small table that functioned as a dining space. She found a match and soon the room was bathed in light. Manuel tossed and turned on the tiny cot that rested beside the bed holding both his brothers, who were still sound asleep. Manuel's face was bright red, sweat clearly visible. Victoria pressed her hand to his face and found it hot to the touch.

"Antonio! Fabian! Wake up!"

In short order, Victoria had a wet cloth from the bucket kept by the door and was cleaning Polonia's face and the covers of her bed. Baby Jesusa woke, crying, unsure what was happening. The two younger boys sat up and rubbed their eyes. Manuel did not move, no matter how many times Victoria called his name.

"Antonio, I need you to find Uncle Pete. He is still camped over in the meadow with the big band of sheep. Do you know it?"

"Yes, Mama. What's wrong?"

"I cannot explain. Just go—take the lantern, it's dark."

Another fit of coughing from Manuel sent Victoria scurrying. He had kicked the thin blanket off his bed during the night, so she retrieved it and covered him tightly, tucking the material snugly around him. She lit a second lantern, the one they kept in the cupboard with Victor's gun, just for emergencies. Then she began to pray.

Dawn was breaking when Antonio returned with Pete. He helped her move Polonia and Manuel to one bed and asked the other three children to sit at the table while Victoria finished cleaning the bedding. They took turns sitting by the sick bed and taking the three healthy children out for fresh air, trying to keep them entertained and quiet. Time passed slowly.

By nightfall, Polonia seemed better. She was still somewhat feverish but exhibited no further vomiting and no cough. Manuel's cough had subsided, and he lay perfectly still, his face glistening with sweat, his skin flushed and clammy to the touch. He woke only rarely.

"If he is no better in the morning, we had better take him into town," Pete said.

Pete and the other children slept fitfully through the night. Victoria sat awake in a chair next to Manuel's cot, her father's pocket watch in her hands, muttering prayers, crossing her fingers to ward off evil spirits, and crying when the fear became too great.

Dawn came. Manuel no longer responded to conversation, nor could his mother wake him with her touch. Victoria and Pete decided it was time to see the doctor. Pete hitched the horses to the buckboard while Victoria gathered the children and a few things they might need. They would head straight for the hotel in Austin where Pete said the doctor made regular visits for just such emergencies. She could leave the other children with a friend in town, she thought, and focus her energies on Manuel. As they climbed aboard the wagon, Manuel resting in the back where Pete had made a bed of blankets, Victoria noticed her father's watch was no longer ticking. She wound the stem and shook it fiercely, holding it to her ear. Nothing.

"Something bad is going to happen," she said to Pete as he settled on the seat beside her and took up the horsewhip. "Go quickly."

***

Victor Rubianes stared deep into his wife's eyes as they sat in silence across the table from one another. He was looking for any sign of emotion, some hint that the woman he had fallen in love with more than a decade ago was still sane. She stared back, implacable.

"*Vitori*," Victor began with a sigh. "Dear one, Manuel has been dead for two months. In all that time you have barely spoken, you have barely bathed, you do not move from this stone cabin. You have other children, *Vitori*. Have you forgotten them?"

Victoria shook her head slowly.

"I remember."

"Good!" said Victor. "Then it is time. I want you and the children to move to Austin, so the boys can go to school. I am making more money than ever now that I am foreman of the Grass Valley Ranch. Juan Saval trusts me with his cattle, his sheep, and his crops. We have hundreds of dollars in the bank now, *Vitori*. You can live in town and finally have a good life."

This time Victoria nodded, but the movement came just as slowly. Victor could not be sure if she understood.

"Say something, dear one. Say you will move to town and spend your time bouncing our daughters on your lap while our sons go to school."

"Not all our sons . . ."

Victor banged his fist on the table once, extremely hard.

"Fine! Not all our sons. You can visit *Manolo*'s grave every day if you live in Austin. His tombstone will be here from Reno this week—you can go and put flowers on it. But you and the children who lived are moving to town. They need you."

Victor stood up with such force that his chair tipped over. He glanced once at the broken pocket watch that Victoria now wore as a necklace every day, swore under his breath, and stomped out the front door.

***

For the few short weeks that the family lived in a fine rental house just off the main street in Austin, Victoria seemed to improve. Every morning she sent the boys off to school, packed the girls in a wheelbarrow, and walked the mile out of town to Manuel's grave. As time dragged on, she started going to the cemetery every other

morning. Then a week went by without a visit to the grave; then two. Meanwhile, death had descended on the town of Austin as other families began to experience the loss of sons and daughters from the raging epidemic. One Sunday morning in early November, Victoria told Fabian she wanted him to check on the family across the street. Pete, who since Manuel's death had given over most of his time to driving the doctor around Lander County on missions of mercy, had said they had the influenza.

"Just knock and stand on the doorstep to talk," she told Fabian. "Do not go inside."

Fabian wandered over to the neighbors at a leisurely pace. He promptly forgot his mother's instructions and, when no one answered the locked front door, went around to the kitchen entrance and let himself in. Inside, he encountered an eerie silence, broken only by the ticking of a clock on the kitchen table. He suddenly remembered his mother's instructions and ran screaming back home.

"They are all dead!" he screeched, breathless from the run.

Victoria shoved all four children in one bedroom, closed the door, and ran to the neighbor's house. She found the family taken to their beds—most unconscious, but not yet dead. She managed to wake one of the children and promised to send the doctor. When she returned home, Victor had arrived on horseback. He was sitting outside on the stoop with Jesusa on his lap. His countenance was grim as he caught her eye.

She saw the look on his face and began at once to cry. She took Jesusa in her arms.

"Someone has died! I can tell by your face. Who is it? Is it Pete? Tell me what has happened!" Still clutching Jesusa, she frantically raced inside and wrapped her arms around her other three children. Victor followed her into the house, shaking his head.

"Juan Saval has been killed in a car accident," he announced. "His widow does not wish to stay at the ranch and his brother asks that you move to the ranch to be the cook. The boys can continue their education—the Savals have a school for a few children in that valley."

Victoria stared at her husband in silence.

"*Vitori*, will you come? It will be a good life. We can save even more money."

Her right hand fluttered up to clasp the pocket watch dangling around her neck. At age 30, she still wore it like a talisman, although she feared its magical powers had dissipated when the ticking stopped. Victoria gave a heavy sigh. Then she spoke in a strong voice Victor had not heard in months.

"Of course, I will come, my husband," she said. "I do not care about the money. I cannot live with all this sickness and death. We need the clean air of the country. It is time for things to be better."

PART THREE:
Land of Opportunity
1920–1933

ELADIA
August 1920
Battle Mountain, Nevada

Eladia stepped unsteadily from the railcar, one hand gripping the side of the door while the other held Maria Luisa's hand. She urged her two-year-old daughter to step lively as they reached the board-covered platform beneath a shabby wooden roof—the sum total of the train station in North Battle Mountain, Nevada. Five miles outside the tiny town of Battle Mountain, the train platform was surrounded by desert. The hot August air felt dry and stale. Eladia tried not to turn up her nose as she surveyed the bleak surroundings, drier and more desolate than any place she had ever visited in Spain. She called over her shoulder to instruct her brother, Eduardo, to be sure little Jesus was off the train, even as she turned her attention toward her other children.

"Pilar! Trinidad! Do not run so fast!"

Her daughters, aged six and five, had quickly leapt from the train ahead of Eladia and Eduardo, and were now pushing their way to the front of a short line of passengers who had disembarked. The girls were eager to find their father, who had promised in a telegram he would meet their train.

"Papa!" cried Pilar, the first to spy Marcelino leaning against a post at the end of the platform. The young girl raced ahead, Trinidad in tow, and both threw themselves into their father's waiting arms.

"Get the bags," Eladia snapped at Eduardo as he joined her on the platform, leading a struggling and uncooperative Jesus by the arm. "Jesus! You stay with me and stop your wiggling."

Eduardo eyed his sister cautiously but said nothing. Catching Marcelino's eye, he jerked his head in greeting before heading to the rear of the train to collect the luggage.

The voyage from Spain had not been easy. A week at sea, every day of which found 24-year-old Eladia more seasick that the one before, had left 16-year-old Eduardo to care for his nieces and nephew. Then came the arrival in New York, with its confusing immigration rules and another kind of sea—this one of people speaking languages Eladia did not understand. Thanks to Eduardo's limited French and the few words of English he had picked up on the ocean liner, they somehow made it through all the lines and checkpoints. The train ride across America was easier, but marred by a lurching motion that reminded Eladia of her seasickness. Now firmly on the ground, she carefully placed one foot in front of the other, walking toward the husband she had not seen in nearly a year. She suddenly felt queasy and looked for a trash can in case she lost the meager contents of her stomach.

Marcelino distracted her with a hug and numerous kisses all over her face. Embarrassed, she pushed him away and bit out a warning to her daughters for running ahead.

"Pilar, take your brother's hand. And you, Trinidad, you are to watch Maria Luisa, so she does not become frightened."

Marcelino laughed and made googly eyes at his children, sharing a moment with them from which Eladia was excluded. Eduardo arrived, weighed down with luggage, and forestalled any reaction from his sister by greeting Marcelino.

"Welcome to America!" called Marcelino as he embraced his young brother-in-law. "And thank you for watching over my chickens these last weeks."

Eduardo drew himself up to his full height and smiled to acknowledge the compliment.

"Weeks?" muttered Eladia. "A year, more like."

Marcelino had in fact left his family in Vitoria-Gasteiz in September 1919, after two frustrating years trying to make the tavern business a success. He had used the last of the American gold earned a decade before to return to Nevada, arriving in Reno with only 35 cents in his pocket. Thanks to the tight network of Basques in the region, he found work as a sheepherder in the mountains near Elko. Eladia, left to tend the tavern, had been instructed to sell the business and follow as soon as she could. She had dragged her feet as long as possible before finally giving up and making the leap. Her mother, who still barely spoke to her eldest daughter, had insisted Eduardo accompany Eladia for safety's sake. Now, standing in the hot Battle Mountain sun, she wondered if she should plan to return to Spain when her brother did.

"Come, come! We have a long journey ahead of us," said Marcelino, ever the lively and enthusiastic one. "There is a truck parked right over there, the blue one, see it girls? We are taking that truck to the Boyer Ranch to see your Aunt Tomasa and Uncle Ramon. Last one in the truck is a spoiled codfish, left in the fisherman's net for the cats to eat!"

His challenge elicited screams of delight and all four children hurtled in the direction of the waiting vehicle.

"Does everything have to be a game with you?" Eladia asked, her voice sounding wearier with each word.

"Nothing wrong with a game, so long as you win!" replied her husband. He slapped his brother-in-law on the back and then linked his arm with Eladia's and marched her toward their new life.

***

Eladia found life at the Boyer Ranch in northern Dixie Valley surprisingly relaxing. Her sister-in-law, Tomasa, had made a comfortable home there for her family. Felix now had a brother, Ramon Jr., and a sister, Maria. The Erquiaga and Arrizabalaga cousins quickly became good friends, and there were many hours of playtime on the sprawling ranch.

Marcelino and Tomasa's younger brothers, David and Pedro, also lived at the Boyer Ranch. The two bachelors worked hard supporting their brother-in-law by leading cattle drives to and from the town of Fallon, a day's ride away in Lahontan Valley.

The ranch had its own reservoir for watering the crops, and within the first month Trinidad fell into the water and nearly drowned. This accident still loomed large for Eladia when Marcelino and Tomasa sat her down and pitched their idea for opening a school.

"Nevada law requires five children to have a school, Ladi," Tomasa explained. "With Pilar, Trinidad, and Jesus—and my two oldest—now we can ask the government to give us a school. It will be important for our children, who are going to be Americans their whole lives."

Eladia did not object to the notion of school, but Marcelino was scheduled to leave for Fallon soon, to accept a job running a ranch for his American patron, George Williams. At first, she did not understand how the two plans could be reconciled. Then it hit her.

"You want me to leave my children here."

Marcelino and Tomasa exchanged nervous glances.

"Yes, Eladia, that is the best plan," said Marcelino after a long pause. "You, me, and Maria Luisa will move to Fallon. The other children will stay here with Tomasa and their cousins so there can be a school. The Boyer Ranch is just not big enough for all of us."

Tomasa tried an encouraging smile. "I will watch over them like my own."

Eladia did not mention the incident with Trinidad and the reservoir. She bit her tongue to keep from pointing out that Tomasa had lost a baby some years before, and that the youngest of Marcelino's siblings, Zacarias, lay buried in a cemetery 100 miles away, having died from typhus in 1915. The logical side of her brain knew that all those events were happenstance, and were in no way Tomasa's fault, but her heart nonetheless felt heavy.

"Can Eduardo come with us?" she whispered, looking deep into her husband eyes.

"Yes, of course!" Marcelino said with enthusiasm. "He will work with me on the ranch in Fallon until he decides it's time to return to Spain, if he ever does."

He paused.

"Please, Ladi," he said in quiet voice. "We have lived apart for a year. I need you with me, and the children need an education."

Eladia made the sign of the cross. It was decided.

VICTORIA

October 1920

Grass Valley Ranch, Nevada

Once more, Victor sat down with his wife and looked her in the eye. What he said caused her jaw to drop.

"What do you mean we have to move?" she asked.

Victoria looked at Victor expectantly. She willed him to say something encouraging, to put a happier face on the grim picture he had just painted.

"The economy is no good," he said instead. "The Savals cannot afford us, according to the estate administrator, and so we are going to have to find a new place. They have already sold the sheep. I have written to the mine superintendent down in Ione. I hear they have work for muckers there."

"Muckers? What does that word mean?"

Victor laughed, despite the circumstances of their conversation. "I don't know, exactly. You work underground. All I know is, if they have work, I am going to take it. You and the children should start packing."

Victoria took a deep breath. She had thought things were going well. They had been at the Grass Valley Ranch for almost two years. From the time the Great War had ended in November 1918, the Rubianeses' bank account had grown. A mild winter had made life easier for everyone at the ranch. In the spring of 1919, Victor went to Austin one day and came back to the ranch the next morning driving a new Model T automobile. The children were ecstatic. Victoria clucked her tongue disapprovingly, growing angry when Victor told her what the car had cost.

"Why would you spend almost a thousand dollars on such a thing?" she asked.

Victor laughed. "Don't be such a stick in the mud! It is the first of its kind in Austin. Look—it has a self-starter! No crank to turn!"

Victoria's frown thawed into a smile, and she returned to her kitchen to bake a berry pie in celebration. Victor barely heard her muttering, "Oh, well, I didn't know it had a self-starter . . . whatever that is." He laughed and took his daughters for their first ride.

There had been, in Victoria's estimation, only one flaw in all their time in Grass Valley.

As the summer of 1920 had dragged on, Victoria learned that her friends, the Barrencheas in Austin, had lost a young child to rabies. The disease was rampant in the area that summer, an epidemic having gripped the state for months. Coyotes coming in from the hills would bite livestock, and the farm animals in turn would become rabid. Consequently, Victor had to shoot much of the ranch's stock. Apparently, the Barrencheas' house cat had become infected and scratched their little girl. A letter from her friends told Victoria the baby had been buried near Manuel. It was too much for Victoria.

"I want every cat on this farm to be shot," she had told Victor. "The children are never to go outside alone, always in pairs, and Antonio must carry a gun when they go without one of us. I am not losing another child, not to the influenza and not to rabies."

When the school year started up, Polly—as Polonia now insisted she be called—started school with her brothers. Little Jesusa was kept in the house, all but tied to her mother's apron strings. The children found they loved the small one-room school. Antonio shortened his name to Tony, following the family pattern of trying to sound more American. Life had seemed to return to normal.

Yet here was Victor disrupting their lives with talk of the economy and moving again. Victoria made the sign of the cross and reached for the chain around her neck.

"Stop that!" Victor ordered. "There are no evil spirits. We are not cursed. There's just no work. It's called a 'depression' the paper says, and it's because the war is over, and all those soldiers don't have jobs. But we are going to be fine."

Victoria had no concept of what a "depression" was, and thus wasn't so sure that the family would be fine, but she knew her husband would not enjoy working underground in a mine for long.

When the Model T was loaded for the trip to Ione, she carefully boxed those items they would need immediately and held them separate from things that could stay in storage for a while.

"I have a funny feeling we won't need everything where we are going," she told Victor.

ELADIA

June 1921

Fallon, Nevada

Eladia shifted uncomfortably in the wooden rocking chair. Between the ache in her back and the baby kicking in her belly, she was having difficulty finding any position that felt at all comfortable. The summer heat did not help. Neither, for that matter, did Marcelino's mood.

"I told you, Eladia, I will go and get the children as soon as I finish this crop of hay," he told her, his tone ringing with impatience. "It takes time."

"Time?" Eladia asked. "How much time have they been away? How much time have I been alone here on this little ranch with only Maria Luisa to keep me company? It's time to bring Pilar, Trinidad, and Jesus home!" She winced from the pain in her back and reached around to place a hand on her hip as she rocked the chair faster and faster.

While her older children had remained at the Boyer Ranch with their relatives so they could attend school, time had passed slowly for Eladia on the ranch owned by successful businessman George Williams. It was Williams who had given Marcelino so many opportunities in America, and this one was no different. The ranch came with a furnished house, six sheep, two cows, two horses, a flock of turkeys, and a pig—far more than they could have bought on their own. Eladia's wealthy upbringing left her feeling a bit smug that the ranch had passed to Williams when the Fallon Socialist Colony failed to create its workers' utopia on the site. She might now be poor herself, but she hated Socialists. Still, she had to admit the ranch afforded a good living, although for Eladia it was a lonely one.

"I said I will go get them, and I will go get them," an exasperated Marcelino said as he strode away from the yard where Eladia sat in her rocking chair, the toddler not far from her feet playing with a rag doll and some uncooked pinto beans from the larder.

Eladia watched him go and only grew angrier. She had not seen her children since their Christmas celebration, a humble affair held at the Boyer Ranch. She and her sister-in-law Tomasa had managed to scrounge together some nuts and candy, making something the Americans called a "popcorn ball," as meager gifts for the young Erquiaga and Arrizabalaga clans. She knew her children were benefiting from the English instruction being provided by the widowed schoolteacher, Mrs. Clara Nauser. But she resented their absence more and more.

"I hope you remember that another mouth to feed will soon be here!" she called after Marcelino. "I will need my daughters' help with the baby, or you won't have any food on your table!"

Marcelino waved his right hand over his head without looking back.

"You see that, Maria Luisa?" Eladia said to her youngest. "He walks away. You will never walk away from your mother like that, will you?"

The toddler responded by picking up her doll and running after her father.

Eladia sighed, finding it hard not to feel emotionally stung by the child's abandonment. At least Eduardo had decided to stay in America. Eduardo's letter home to their parents in Spain informing them of his decision had gone unanswered, further evidence that Nicanor and Francisca blamed Marcelino for their children's ill-fated decisions. But for Eladia, it meant that she felt somewhat less isolated, while for Marcelino, it meant that he had help tending to the little ranch, at least for now. Unfortunately, Eduardo had begun to make noises about finding his own fortune as soon as he turned 18, which undoubtedly meant he, too, would wander out of Eladia's life sooner rather than later. She tried not to think about that.

The tired woman rose with some difficulty from the rocking chair and looked around her. The yard was dirt, without so much as a fence. The tiny house had no indoor plumbing and not much of a kitchen. More often than not, she cooked outside on an open fire.

So much for the Land of Opportunity, she thought. For a moment she was lost in memories of chauffeur-driven cars, Christmas sweets, ball gowns, and even the endless hours of piano practice.

Another twinge in her belly reminded her there was one thing that would be more pleasant in this country. She was scheduled to deliver her baby, due in early July, at what passed for a hospital in the town of Fallon. In Spain, all her children had been born at home with a midwife in attendance. Marcelino had already borrowed checks from a friend to pay the hospital and doctor each one hundred dollars. They would reimburse the friend in cash when the summer's hay sold. At least that much was arranged.

Still, she wanted her children close by. Not out of fear for their safety, but because Eladia was lonely. With no one except her husband and brother to talk to, she had learned almost no English in nearly a year, and she had no real desire to do so. She longed for things that felt Spanish—and for the lively existence in a city like Vitoria-Gasteiz, where there were shops and parks and churches, with a bus system and a vibrant Old City. Fallon had a population of just a few hundred people, and its main thoroughfare—named Maine Street for the founder's home state, in a pun that was lost on the Spaniards—offered little by way of entertainment or shopping.

Eladia felt a tug at the hem of her worn blue cotton dress. She looked down and forced a smile at Maria Luisa as another pain pulsed through her belly.

"Your new brother or sister will be here before we know it, Maria. We had better sweep the house."

She was surprised when Maria Luisa agreed with a loud "Yes!" in English. Maybe they were becoming Americans after all.

***

Little Antonio Manuel arrived just a week before his siblings were driven into Fallon by Uncle Ramon, and Eladia was already back home to greet them. Although the nation had been living under the rules of Prohibition for over a year, Marcelino had friends who ran "bootleg" stills in the desert surrounding Fallon's many small ranches. He procured a bottle of gin and invited the neighbors to a picnic in the yard of the little ranch. While Eladia rested in her rocking chair, her husband regaled the group with stories of his time as a young sheepherder in the wilds of Nevada.

"One day I was riding my horse, minding my own business, when—you will never guess what happened," Marcelino said, pausing to take another drink.

"You broke your back!" Pilar shouted.

Everyone laughed, including Eladia. The group was so familiar with Marcelino's excellent stories—all of them one part truth and one part fable—that almost anyone present could have offered the ending of this tale.

Marcelino joined in the laughter. "That's right, my little daughter. I was thrown from my horse and landed on a rock. My back was broken—well, maybe not the bones, but something broke—and I could not use my arms! For the rest of that winter, I could walk along with the sheep, but my arms hung useless by my sides. The other sheepherders had to dress me and feed me . . ."

"Like a baby!" offered Pilar, racing to her mother's side, and patting her baby brother on the head perhaps a little too vigorously.

"Yes, yes! Just like little Antonio here," Marcelino said with a smile. He took another drink.

Eladia eyed her husband's liquor consumption with some concern, yet she had to admit, the storytelling reminded her of the man who had cajoled her into marriage with his tales of the American West and his sense of humor. She rocked her chair a bit more and then leaned forward.

"Tell them about arriving in Reno with . . ." She paused and looked at Pilar.

"Thirty-five cents in your pocket!" mother and daughter said in dramatic unison.

Marcelino slapped his knee and took a breath, ready for the tale. Eladia smiled and kissed her baby on the head.

VICTORIA
September 1921
Paradise Valley, Nevada

Victor Rubianes had at long last applied for American citizenship. He and Victoria had continued the alien registration every year of their marriage, but his initial steps toward citizenship were emblematic of the family's new level of comfort with their lives. Victoria could feel herself begin to relax as they had settled into life back in Paradise Valley, the mines of Ione having proved—as she suspected—a short-lived experiment. Feeling at home once again in the town of Paradise, Victor had taken the first step toward becoming an American citizen by filing paperwork declaring an intention for naturalization.

The only worry, and it was a constant one, was Fabian's breathing problem. He had what the visiting doctor from Winnemucca called "asthma," and it made him extremely weak. It had begun in the spring when he suffered a bout of diphtheria so severe all his hair fell out. The doctor said the diphtheria had something to do with shallow wells and outdoor toilets too close to the buildings in town, but the malady had passed. The asthma, however, was a permanent condition. The doctor said it could be managed, but Victoria worried nonetheless, remembering Manuel's coughing and shortness of breath before he died. She had kept Fabian home from school as much as she could when the fall term began.

When he did go to school, Fabian liked to tease Jesusa—who was not yet school age—for being afraid of the very idea of school and its frightening principal. Victoria smiled as she listened to the latest tale he had brought home from school.

"Old Man Hampton has this peg leg, see, and one real leg, and today when he came into class, the floors had just been polished, so the wood on his peg leg slipped, and he fell down!"

Everyone chuckled at the story except Victor, who sat quietly at the table and rubbed his stomach.

"Stomach still hurting?" Victoria asked. "It's been over a week."

Victor nodded. "Nothing to worry about. Gas, I suspect."

That night, Victor began to vomit blood, and he was forced to admit his bowels had not moved in several days. The next day, a trip to Reno was arranged by Victor's brother, Jenaro, whom the children called "Uncle Joe." Victoria stayed home with the children, and a few days later, Joe returned with word that Victor had a bowel obstruction and had undergone emergency surgery. The physician had drained more than a gallon of fluid from his abdomen and removed the blockage.

"The doctor says it is very serious, *Vitori*, but it's nothing to do with your cooking," Joe said. "Vic wanted me to say that." He offered a weak smile.

Victoria grumbled at the joke about her cooking, but she was more worried that her husband might not return. *Men and boys who go to town to see the doctor . . . well, it doesn't end well*, she thought.

Her worries were interrupted by screams of glee when Uncle Joe produced two baby dolls, complete with doll-size baby buggies, which he had procured in Reno for Polly and Jesusa. The girls begged their mother to take them to the town dance at the hotel that night so they could show off their new treasures. Dolls and dancing proved a welcome distraction.

***

Victor returned home three weeks later, still pale, and considerably thinner than the family remembered, and it was decided he needed to spend the long winter in his bed. Once more, he was out of work. Victoria rallied—finding income from friends who needed sewing, and augmenting what little she could buy with food their friends sent over from the hotel—but one day in early spring 1922, she was faced with a startling fact: all the money was gone.

"Antonio, Fabian, I need you to go out into the fields again and pick some young dandelions. Your father needs a salad for his dinner, and I have two eggs I am going to boil and serve with the greens."

The boys whined and made a big show of protesting this injustice. It was not the work they minded as much as the fact that they were sick of dandelions. They, too, realized that the eggs were the last real food in the house.

"Take your sisters with you. Everyone needs some air," Victoria announced.

With the children out of the house, she went to Victor's bedside. He spent more time in bed than anywhere, it seemed, but they rarely had the house to themselves.

"Victor, what are we going to do? I am running out of ideas."

Victor nodded. "There is nothing left but prayer, I think, or your magic pocket watch," he said and reached for the tarnished necklace that hung around his wife's neck.

"Gimme dis," he said with a smile.

Victoria slapped his hand away. But she removed the chain from around her neck and handed over the watch. "I suggest you pray very hard," she said, and returned to the kitchen to prepare the last of the eggs.

The letter arrived the next day.

John Hickison of Dry Creek, outside Austin, wrote to say he fondly remembered Victor from his days at Grass Valley. Hickison had taken over the Kingston Ranch in the Big Smoky Valley and he thought Victor would be the perfect man to run the place. His letter offered terms of taking the ranch "on shares," meaning the Rubianeses would not be paid a salary but would keep a portion of proceeds from any produce sold and have all the food from the ranch for their own use. Hickison needed a reply soon because he wanted Victor installed by the end of summer.

In short order, everything went into the Model T except the two baby buggies, for which there was no room. Jesusa and Polly cried for their loss all the way to Kingston. Victoria made certain the pocket watch was safely hanging from its chain around her neck, convinced it had worked a miracle.

ELADIA
January 1923
Fallon, Nevada

Winter was Eladia's least favorite time of the year. It seemed she felt cold year-round, but ice and snow made her bones ache. The house that came with the Franke Ranch, which Marcelino and Eladia were renting for fifty dollars a month, had no insulation. What had seemed passable when they moved to the place in the summer of 1922 was now unbearable. Eladia had to rub her hands together to keep her fingers warm enough to operate the used treadle sewing machine Marcelino brought home as a Christmas present. It was a far cry from the Singer sewing machines that had first brought the young couple together, but it did the job—when she could keep her fingers warm long enough.

At her feet, young Antonio played with a few old and worn toys. Because the family had no money for such frivolities, the Erquiaga children regularly scavenged the Fallon dump, located about half a mile from the Franke place, for toys that other families had thrown out."How does your nose feel?" Eladia asked the boy, who was just 18 months old.

The toddler merely breathed through his mouth and smiled.

Jesus and Antonio had been playing cowboys on Christmas Day when the game got too rough. Antonio was "bucked off" his older brother, who had obligingly been playing the role of horse to Antonio's cowboy. His face hit the kitchen floor, and his nose had been broken. A trip to town two days later yielded an expensive proposal from the doctor to reset the nose, but as the Erquiagas had spent the last of their money on the sewing machine, they demurred. Antonio's broken bone was not set, and for the last three weeks, Eladia watched as the bruising faded and the nose remained flat and bent to one side.

"Maybe some music will make you forget the pain," said Eladia.

Still rubbing her hands for warmth, she left the sewing machine and walked to the phonograph by the window. Marcelino had purchased this device, which required the frequent turning of a handle to keep the music playing, about a year before when they had a few extra dollars. The family had no radio, so the phonograph and a few records that came with it helped to pass the time. Eladia favored the waltzes which reminded her of piano lessons and parties at her parents' home. She selected one by Strauss, gave the handle a few turns, and was headed back to her sewing when Pilar burst into the house from outside.

"Papa has been in an accident!"

Eladia made the sign of the cross. "What now?" she asked.

Pilar, out of breath from running all the way home from town in the biting cold, explained that she, Jesus, and Marcelino had taken the wagon and horse team into Fallon. Something spooked the horses, and they were all thrown from the wagon. The children, who had been riding in the wagon bed, were unhurt, but their father had landed on a barbed wire fence beside the road. Concerned about the extent of his injuries, Marcelino had caught a ride with a neighbor into town, leaving Jesus with the wagon while Pilar ran home.

"He said he was going to the hospital," Pilar said, her voice cracking and her eyes filling with tears. "There was a lot of blood, Mama!"

"Oh, I'm sure he will be fine," said Eladia. "Sit here with Antonio while I find your sisters and decide what is to be done." She donned a coat and walked outside.

Trinidad and Maria Luisa were out in the makeshift barn, cleaning up from that morning's milking chores. Eladia, who could not drive the one truck the family owned, told Trinidad to run to the Getto family's house up the road and ask for someone to come take them to the hospital. She returned to the house with Maria Luisa and tried again in vain to get warm while she waited for Mr. Getto to arrive.

Pilar was worried about her father.

"Mama, how will you pay the hospital? Papa will need to have his cuts sewed up," she whined.

Eladia snorted. "If we can't pay for Antonio's nose, we can't pay for sewing up your father's cuts," she said, a note of bitterness in her voice. "Maybe he can use the sewing machine."

Pilar cried even more at this idea, which set off Maria Luisa's tears and caused Trinidad's upper lip to quiver. An exasperated Eladia said a silent prayer before deciding to take pity on her daughters.

"Where is that record you like so much?"

Eladia looked through the stack of records and found the one she had seen her children play over and over. She could not read the song title, since it was in English, but she recognized the color of the small round label in the center of the disc. The record was soon in place, and she was spinning up the phonograph when Mr. Getto drove into the yard.

"Be good and take care of Antonio," Eladia told the girls. She dropped the needle in place and walked out the door as Pilar and Trinidad began to snicker and dance around the room. Maria Luisa and Antonio clapped their hands as Trinidad sang out the chorus.

"You made a chicken out of your mother, but you won't make a goose of me!"

Pilar was laughing so hard she nearly fell to the floor.

VICTORIA
October 1925
Kingston, Nevada

Victoria stood in the kitchen of the Kingston Ranch house, gazing out the window at the plum and apple trees that dotted the yard. A large tub of water rested on the counter before her. She was washing dishes, enjoying the feel of the warm water on her hands. She found herself smiling and gave a little chuckle.

October had arrived with a snap of cold in the air, christening the arrival of fall and the anniversary of the family's time at the mouth of Kingston Canyon. Three years had passed since the family arrived at the Kingston Ranch, all their belongings—save the doll buggies—tucked in the Model T. It had taken some getting used to, living so far out of Austin; the only people nearby were a Native American family who lived in a tent by the creek about two miles up the canyon, and the forest ranger who lived with his family a little farther on.

Tony had spent the first year living with the Dory family, a day's horse ride away. They had a school building at the Dorys' ranch, and four children, but Nevada law required five children to sustain a school, so Tony had been loaned to the Dory clan for several months. But the next year, Tony was brought home. Victor had petitioned the Nevada Superintendent of Public Instruction for his own school at Kingston and asked the nearby Native American family to send their two children to school with the four Rubianes kids to meet the state's quota. School supplies—consisting of a blackboard, student desks, and textbooks—had been purchased from the Myers Ranch in nearby Blackbird Canyon, where a school had gone defunct, and Victor became clerk of the new Smoky Valley School.

Two teachers had come and gone in as many years, and Victoria had liked each one better than the last. She also recognized the benefits her children were receiving from their American education. Even her own English was improving. The family still chuckled at the experience with the first teacher, an elderly lady from San Francisco who had been raised in Boston. Fabian had quickly become a perfect mimic of her Boston-educated accent, frequently offering his siblings the sum of a "dollar and a *hawlf* for a cow and a *cawlf*." Victor and Victoria had laughed right along with their children.

Food was as plentiful as laughter, another change from the lean days in Paradise Valley. Life in Kingston was filled with fruits and vegetables from the garden, fresh beef and lamb from the fields, and staples such as flour and sugar purchased or bartered from the store in Austin three or four times a year when the family would make the trek into town. Plums from the orchard and elderberries from Kingston Canyon yielded pies, jams, and jellies. Apples and potatoes could be put away in the cellar for winter or sold at market. Cabbages were a cash crop as well. The hogs, animals so vile that Victor would often feed them the carcass of a cow or deer lost to disease, provided both food and cash for the Rubianes family.

Victoria still found ways to sew her family's clothing, often from the flour sacks they procured in town, and this task kept her busy as the four children were all growing taller, with ruddy cheeks and ever-present smiles. Victor had experienced no further health problems and spent many an evening playing cards with his young brood and regaling them with tales of Spain. The children were hale and hearty. Fabian, and his mother, had grown used to his asthma. Even Manuel's death was a fading memory.

Yes, it is a good life, Victoria thought as she looked out the window. She chuckled at the fond memories in Kingston, wiped her hands on her apron, and walked outside to see what trouble the children might be in now. Little Jessie, formerly Jesusa, who had Americanized her name just as her older sister had done, nervously greeted Victoria in the orchard.

"Mom, something is wrong with Tony," Jessie said. "His words are all jumbled and he's holding his stomach like Pop used to do in Paradise."

Victoria broke into a dead run, headed straight for the bunkhouse where the boys slept.

"Find your father!" she screamed over her shoulder as she ran.

In the bunkhouse, Tony was stumbling around the room and mumbling while his brother tried to take him by the arm and get him to take a seat on the bed.

"Tony, just relax and sit down. You're not making any sense," Fabian was saying.

"What's wrong with him?" Victoria shouted. Fabian stepped back and looked at his mother as if she had slapped him.

"Mom, he's not making any sense," the boy began. "We didn't do nothing—"

"Antonio! Speak to me. What is wrong?" Victoria grabbed her older son by the shoulders and shook him.

"We need to bring in the cabbage before it cracks in the rain," the boy whispered. "And plow the meadow up in the canyon." He touched his forehead before continuing. "Who are you? Where are Mom and Pop?"

Victoria enfolded her son in her arms, frantically rubbing his back as she pressed her cheek against his. She tried to make soothing noises but quickly began to cry uncontrollably. Unsure what to do, Fabian took his sister Polly by the hand and crept away from the bunkhouse, as afraid of his mother's reaction as he was Tony's descent into delirium. Once outside, the two children ran to the schoolhouse across the yard and told the new teacher, Miss Belaustegui, what was happening.

"Stay right here," the young woman said. "Neither of you move an inch."

Victor arrived on the run from the other direction just as the teacher reached the bunkhouse. They exchanged glances as Victoria's wailing grew in both pitch and volume.

"*Madre de Dios*, not again," said Victor.

***

Austin still had no hospital, so once again a Rubianes son lay confined to his bed in a hotel that perched on a side street of the mountain town. Victoria sat in a straight-backed wooden chair next to Tony's bedside with her husband standing next to her, his right hand protectively resting on her shoulder.

"Bleeding ulcers," the doctor pronounced. "Your boy has bleeding ulcers, I believe, and he has lost so much blood that he is delirious and frankly in grave danger."

Neither Victor nor his wife understood the English words "ulcer" or "delirious," so a short conversation ensued as the doctor first tried to explain, then in frustration he summoned the girl from the hotel's reception desk who spoke Basque as well as English. She managed a passable explanation, but not without difficulty.

"Tell them their boy has to be taken to Fallon," the doctor shouted at the young girl, as if the volume of his words would somehow help her make sense of what he was saying. "He needs a hospital." Every syllable of every word was pronounced slowly and with great exaggeration.

"We are not stupid, sir," Victor said in a cold, quiet voice. "I understand the word hospital. How soon can you leave with my boy?"

"It will cost $112—one for every mile from here to Fallon," the doctor said. He did not shout the words for a change.

"That is robbery, sir," Victor ground out.

"We pay," said Victoria in her best English. "We have money. We pay."

She rose from her chair and marched from the room.

It took two days to organize the doctor's trip to Fallon with Tony. During that time, Victoria's brother, Pete, arrived and announced he would take his sister back to the ranch in Kingston. Victor would make the journey to Fallon with the boy.

"Your English is not good enough to manage the doctors," Pete told his anxious and angry sister when she objected to the plan. "And you have three other children fending for themselves at the ranch."

Victoria scowled. "I do not need you and that husband of mine to remind me how many children I have and do not have!" But she returned to Kingston.

Days turned to weeks and weeks stretched into a second full month as Victoria and her children waited. Victor had taken lodging with friends in Fallon, and Tony was slowly recovering at the Fallon hospital. The three younger children, taken to Austin by their mother on the buckboard wagon for church one Sunday, soon regretted "rubbering" on the phone—that is, listening in on their mother's conversation—when they stopped at the priest's house after Mass so Victoria could place the call to Fallon. They learned that Tony had nearly died on more than one occasion. But they were relieved to also overhear that their father and brother would be home by Christmas Day.

***

When the long-awaited holiday came, things in Kingston kicked into high gear. "We must have a feast fit for the Baby Jesus," announced Victoria, immediately regretting her words, and making the sign of the cross to ward off evil. "Fabian, get one of the native boys to help you, and kill a baby pig. I will roast it whole."

In addition to the roasted pig, there were potatoes and carrots from the cellar, fresh-baked bread, an apple pie, and the girls even made ice cream from cream stored in what the family called "the cold house." Victor had diverted some of the water from Kingston Creek through a hole in the floor of a stone building on the ranch. The water kept the family's milk and other perishables cold in the stone house year-round. Ice cream was a rare treat, but Tony's homecoming was worth the effort.

Friends in Paradise Valley had sent boxes of goodies for the family, knowing of their recent troubles. Jessie and Polly had been thrilled to find paper dolls and handmade ornaments for the Christmas tree in the schoolhouse that Miss Belaustegui had insisted they have. The teacher told them how to decorate the tree and helped Victoria prepare the feast for dinner.

Wan and pale, Tony arrived with his father in the Model T in the early afternoon on Christmas Eve. He was soon smiling and chipper, needling his brother about seeming to be shorter than when he and Pop had left for Fallon.

"And you two girls," quipped the returning son. "You've been spending too much time on horseback. Your shanks's ponies are spindly and weak."

The girls giggled obligingly. Tony always referred to their legs as "shanks's ponies," and they both knew it was meant affectionately. No one loved horses more than Tony. He would rather ride a horse than drink water any day of the year. His teasing was a welcome sign.

"Polly, I hear Miss Belaustegui here expelled you from the schoolhouse for a whole week," Tony ribbed. "What did you do wrong this time?"

Polly did not answer, instead staring sheepishly at her shoes. Miss Belaustegui pointed out that Tony, too, had spent a fair amount of time in her detention room behind the bunkhouse before his illness. "People who live in glass houses should not throw stones," she opined. Everyone laughed, especially Polly.

***

With Tony sidelined from strenuous work around the ranch, Fabian became his father's primary workmate as 1926 dawned. Although he was only 14, the boy pitched in wherever he could with the often back-breaking labor of managing the ranch. Victor put Fabian to work dragging the fields with a team of horses and a ten-feet-wide drag constructed of willows from the creek bed. Dragged across the fields before too much of the ground had thawed, the contraption would break up the cow manure and thereby fertilize the ground for spring. The work was more tedious than it was difficult, and Fabian sometimes got bored and wandered off before the task was completed, leaving the horse team tied to a tree.

One day in March, Victor set his son to work with the drag, admonishing him to finish the task before supper, and then headed off to the Smithline Ranch up the road a few miles. By two o'clock, snow had begun to fall. Victoria could see her son in the field from the kitchen window of the house, and she knew he had no gloves for such a cold day. Without hesitation, she retrieved the long white gloves she only wore to church from a hat box on the top shelf of her storage cupboard and trudged across the increasingly snow-covered field to her son. She held the gloves out with both hands, not speaking a word.

Fabian shook his head. "Mom, those are your church gloves. I don't need them. My hands aren't that cold."

Victoria bit her lip.

"I have had enough sick sons," she finally declared. She shoved the gloves at her son, who obediently took them and put the delicate coverings on without a hint of embarrassment before resuming his work. By the time Victor returned, the ranch was covered in so much snow that the dragging had no effect on the manure at all, but Fabian continued to drive the horse team in endless loops around the field. Victor scolded the boy and boxed his ears, but he did not notice the tears in his son's eyes as he removed the once-white gloves, blackened and torn now from the rough leather reins used to the steer the horses.

Victoria made whipped cream for the pudding she prepared that night of rice, steamed milk, and raisins. Victor did not speak up when his bowl of pudding had no whipped cream, while Fabian's had a double serving.

ELADIA

September 1927
Fallon, Nevada

"Trinidad, you should be more careful with the bread! It is the staff of life!"

Eladia was frustrated with her second child. Trinidad was always in a hurry, always flitting from place to place and chore to chore, without sufficient care for the importance of what she had been asked to do. The child had just dropped a freshly baked roll on the floor when she was supposed to be putting them all in a basket for supper that evening.

"Yes, Mama, I know the rules," said the 12-year-old, her bottom lip sticking out.

"Tell me," ordered Eladia.

Trinidad sighed. "We take the bread out of the oven and place it upside down until it has cooled. Then we turn it right side up and carefully place it in the basket. If we drop the bread, we must show it reverence." She kissed the roll she had dropped just seconds before, then placed it carefully—right side up—in the basket with the rest.

Eladia pursed her lips and shook her head. She supposed the recitation of the rules would suffice, but she made a mental note to read her children an extra story from the religious book her sister had sent them from Spain. Perhaps they needed to hear the story of Our Lady of the Pillar, to remind them that Spain—not America—was the place the Blessed Virgin had made her first mystical appearance to mankind. She would also have to remember to admonish her daughters not to sew on Sunday, lest they pierce Saint Mary's heart. She worried her children would stray too far from their Catholic heritage here in a land where Protestants were so plentiful. Marcelino was not much help. He never read religious stories to the children, preferring tales from *Don Quixote* and *One Thousand and One Arabian Nights*.

Eladia found such things frivolous and consistently vowed to push harder for adherence to the rules of the Church.

But for now, she had her hands full caring for Baby Carmen, her seventh child, who had reached her sixteenth day in age today. Eladia still remembered the loss of her fourth child in Spain after only two weeks of life. With each subsequent child she fretted and prayed to the Blessed Virgin to spare her another such loss. Just as with Jose Luis, whose birth had followed Antonio's before Carmen joined the family, her prayers had been answered; Carmen was healthy and always hungry.

"Enough, enough," she said at last to Trinidad, who was still muttering under her breath about the rules for taking care of bread. "We are out of chicken eggs today because I sent them all to market. I need you to find your brother Jesus and go out to the slough and gather duck eggs."

This news brightened Trinidad's outlook considerably. She skipped from the room, leaving the basket of rolls on the kitchen table.

The Erquiagas had moved around Lahontan Valley, the farmland surrounding the town of Fallon, for the last seven years. Their current home, rented as part of yet another sharecropping agreement with a businessman of Marcelino's acquaintance, was a ranch in the lowlands that had largely dried up when the federal government built a dam on the Carson River a decade ago. A slough—essentially a small swamp—remained from the river's original passage, and there was a small island in the middle of the water that was a favorite spot for migrating ducks and geese. The Erquiaga children were often sent there for eggs, a mainstay of the family's diet.

On her good days, Eladia chuckled at how different her life was now, sending a child to forage for food because there was so little money, when in her own youth a driver had taken her to town to shop for ballgowns and lace. On bad days, she resented the changed circumstances.

Today was a good day. The baby was healthy, the bread was baked, and for once the older children were out of her hair. Jose Luis was napping, as was Baby Carmen. Eladia walked to the bedroom she and Marcelino shared with the two youngest children and found the copy of *Lives of the Saints* sent by her sister. Resting on the edge of the bed, she skimmed through the pages for the story of Saint Mary's visit to Saint James the Greater (Santiago to the Spanish). The Lady's feast day was coming up in a few weeks. Maybe Eladia could summon the strength to bake a cake—that is, if she could find any sugar to go with the eggs.

VICTORIA
November 1927
Fallon, Nevada

"Mr. and Mrs. Rubianes, I have good news and bad news," the wizened old doctor said with a wry smile.

Victoria glared at her husband, irritated that he had insisted she join him and their son Tony for a visit to the doctor. On a cold wintery night two weeks prior, as the family relaxed at home, Victoria had been attempting to learn the steps to the complicated Charleston, to the great amusement of her children, when she suddenly felt light-headed and nearly fainted. The feeling persisted over several days before she finally confided in Victor. He had quickly put Victoria in the old Model T with Tony, who was due for a checkup on his ulcer. They made the trek to Tonopah, which, although farther away than Austin, offered a second medical opinion from the doctor in Austin who had charged $112 for the trip to Fallon.

In short order, the doctor in Tonopah had made his inspections of young Tony and his mother, now aged 39.

"First, I think your son's ulcer is so bad that he would benefit from a lower altitude. I think you should consider moving away from the Kingston Canyon. He needs a hospital and a different climate."

Victor and Victoria took each other's hands and stared at the doctor.

"What else?" Victor finally asked. "You said there was good news. We would like to hear that."

The doctor looked at Victoria, a twinkle in his eyes.

"You're going to have a baby, Mrs. Rubianes," he announced. "I believe the child is due in May. You're going to need that hospital as well."

The doctor slapped his knee and laughed as the young couple's jaws dropped in unison.

***

Nearly seven months pregnant, arms akimbo to relieve the pressure in her aching lower back, Victoria stood in the dusty yard of what would be her new home. Victor had leased the Belaustegui Ranch from family members of Miss Belaustegui, the schoolteacher, for $1,000 per year. The ranch, about four miles north of downtown Fallon in Old River District, came with 2 cows, 4 horses, 25 turkey hens, and 2 gobblers. Victor was concerned they knew nothing about raising turkeys, but from Victoria's standpoint, the real trouble was that the ranch did not come with a house, the original residence having burned down a year before.

"You couldn't have been organized enough to move the house before we arrived with all these kids?" she snapped at her husband, who was whipping a team of horses as it pulled a house from a neighboring orchard to the homestead where the Rubianes clan would live. Several neighbors and representatives of the Belaustegui family were on hand to help, giving the event an aura of excitement, but Victoria was not enjoying the day.

The homestead included a well and a pump house; running water would be available outside, as would an outhouse of course. Several farm buildings, including a blacksmith workshop, were in reasonably good shape. The simple house they were relocating had just four rooms. But Victoria's back hurt, and she wanted a place to sleep. She and the children had slept in the car for four days while Victor sorted out the details of moving the house.

She saw her husband glare at her, and she knew he was brooding. Victor was at heart a buckaroo, a cowboy who loved the open range of rural Nevada. He had loved the remoteness of Kingston. He did not understand the kind of farming done at the Belaustegui Ranch, with its flood irrigation and planted alfalfa fields. He did not understand turkeys. He did not want to live this close to a town, with its banks and schools and Fraternal Hall. He had made the move for her and their eldest son, she knew, and it occurred to her that perhaps she ought not push too hard. She turned her ire elsewhere.

"Fabian! Stop teasing your sisters!"

Tomorrow the three younger children would be driven to town to be placed in the large public school, called Oats Park, that Fallon afforded its youngest residents. Tony had graduated from the eighth grade before the family left Kingston, despite an epic battle with Miss Belaustegui about whether he could—or would—draw a picture of a bird for the final exam. Even with the bird undrawn, testament to a stubborn streak that ran deep in the family, Tony had completed the last required grade of public education and thus would go straight to work on the new ranch, while Fabian, Polly, and Jessie would have to attend school in town.

"Wife, your house is complete!" Victor called at last. His pronouncement elicited a smattering of applause from all assembled.

At Oats Park School the next day, Victoria was unable to make sense of the conversation, so the children interpreted for her. Despite the difference in their ages, Polly and Fabian would both be placed in the eighth grade. Fabian had long ago fallen behind because he missed so much school over the years due to his health, but the Kingston teachers had done such good work that Polly would advance one level beyond where she chronologically ought to be. Jessie, meanwhile, was installed in the third-grade class. Victor shook his head at the city folk and their pretensions, but Victoria was thankful the children would be out from under her daily supervision when the baby came.

Right on schedule, little Anita was born on May 28, the first in her family to be born in a hospital. Victor had wanted to name her after his sister, Juanita, but Polly and Jessie had argued their way to Anita, because it sounded more American to them. Although not recorded on her birth certificate, the child's middle name was declared by her sisters to be May, for the month of her birth. Victoria ignored all conversations about the name, fretting instead about the fact that the infant shared a birthday with her dead brother, Manuel. Each day the three Rubianes children walked to the bus stop, a vastly different experience from walking across the yard in Kingston to the one-room schoolhouse on their own ranch. Though novel, bus rides were largely uneventful, while lunches often proved an embarrassment. Victoria sent the children to school with all their food in one big, shared shoe box, with field-hand-sized sandwiches and hard-boiled eggs for each of them. Fabian and Polly had to sit with Jessie in the lower grades to share this communal lunch. Fabian ultimately stopped eating during the day to avoid the embarrassment.

Victor's fears about the turkey farming had already proven correct in the short time they had lived on the ranch. In the first week, he and the boys accidentally flooded the yard due to their lack of understanding of the new irrigation system. Being too stupid to seek out higher ground, several hens died.

"We never should have left Kingston," Victor had said. "I don't understand this farm, I can't put up hay under these conditions, and everything is always flooded by these damn ditches!"

Victoria said nothing in response. She hoped for an improvement in Tony's health, and, despite Victor's complaining about the ranch, he loved the new baby more than anything else in his simple life. He called the girl "Annie" more often than by her given name and had taken to pushing her pram around the yard at night while the boys did his chores for him.

True, food was not as plentiful here as it had been in Kingston, and Victoria had to work harder to sew clothing for her children, who were often embarrassed by their country ways and homemade garb when comparing themselves to children in the town. But at least no one was sick.

"Everything is settling down," Victoria reassured her husband, even as the silences between them stretched from summer to fall and into December. "We will make it through the rest of summer, and everyone in town is saying that 1929 is going to be a good year for farmers. You'll see."

***

The stock market crash of 1929 did not have an immediate effect on the Rubianes family's fortunes. Victor had managed to save money from the sharecropping proceeds and, as the rest of the nation plunged into unemployment, he kept his family clothed and fed thanks to the farm's income and some edible crops. But for Victoria, the momentary respite from worrying had passed. Tony was having trouble finding work in town, and Fabian, having ended his schooling with eighth grade graduation, still had the occasional bout of asthma as he helped Victor with the farm. Victoria marked time on the calendar like a prisoner keeping track of a sentence and became more and more superstitious about bad omens, and more and more watchful of her growing teenagers and their forays into town for dances and school activities.

Christmas that year saw little in the way of joy at the ranch. The children were relieved to be taken to town for the annual Knights of Pythias holiday gathering around the Christmas tree erected on Maine Street. With no presents at home, they waited in the long line for Santa Claus to hand each child a red mesh stocking containing one orange, a few nuts, and five pieces of hard candy. They were overjoyed, their voices rising to near shouts as they compared their gifts.

Victoria's commentary was somewhat bleaker.

"That's all you can expect, since we don't have anything more at home to give you," she warned her brood. "Now get back in the car so we can go home. I'm cold."

Even the usually optimistic Victor made no effort to boost the children's spirits on the short trek northward to the ranch. Instead, he and Victoria talked about the one thing they had become convinced would change their life for the better: owning their own ranch.

"I promise you we are still going to be able to save enough money to buy a place of our own, *Vitori*. I think we need five thousand dollars," Victor said. "That is what the Americans call 'the magic number.' If we can put that much money in the bank, we can buy our own place, I promise. Things will be better then."

ELADIA
April 1931
Fallon, Nevada

Nicanor Aguirre was dead.

The telegram informing Eladia of her father's passing had arrived, ironically and painfully, on her birthday, February 18. Her sister Filomena had sent the news, including a short phrase that confused Eladia at the time: "Everything is different now."

Of course everything is different, she had thought. *Papa is dead of a stroke at the age of 71.* The man who ran Aguirre Enterprises and the Casa Aguirre with the same iron fist would surely leave a void in that family.

The letter from her mother arrived two months later.

Eladia had read the letter over so many times she could recite parts of it from memory. Francisca Aguirre de Arroyabe was extending an olive branch. If Eladia and her seven children would return to Spain, all would be forgiven. She was instructed to bring her brother Eduardo as well. The eldest brother, Mauricio, had been placed in charge of the family's business holdings. With Nicanor barely installed in the family tomb outside Nanclares, the surviving matriarch of his clan had apparently taken charge.

No mention of Marcelino was made in the letter.

Eladia knew the omission signaled that she was expected to leave her husband in America and return to Spain with her brother and children, just as they had left. Her sons Antonio and Jose Luis, and daughter Carmen, had been added to the family since that transatlantic journey in 1920, but they were as welcome as Pilar, Trinidad, Jesus, and Maria Luisa—who were all Spanish citizens by birth.

She wondered if she could really do it. She had been sitting at the kitchen table for over an hour, staring into a cup of coffee long gone cold, her fingers worrying the edges of Filomena's original telegram and her mother's letter. The small kitchen had running water and a stove, a marked improvement over some of the places the Erquiagas had lived in during the decade they had moved around Fallon. This was the third—no, fourth—little ranch Marcelino had leased on shares, yet another scheme to get rich off someone else's land, and so far, it had gone just as poorly as all the others. Yes, Marcelino had built up a small herd of dairy cows and a band of sheep, but that was virtually all they owned. Each succeeding house came with furniture, so they purchased almost nothing. Eladia's little flock of chickens never grew to any great size, its members regularly eaten by a family that lived on the edge of hunger most of the time.

Eladia considered just how much money her family in Spain possessed. True, Spain was suffering from the same ill effects as America following the stock market crash of 1929. But Mauricio would still inherit control of a fortune, not a flock of chickens. Francisca had made that clear.

Eladia compared her family's prospects to the days she would send Jesus into town with 10 cents for a soup bone from the butcher, or the countless times she would try to barter with shop clerks on Maine Street, speaking through her daughters. "Offer them 79 cents," she would say when eying an item priced at a dollar. No matter how many times her daughters told her that Americans did not barter like the Spanish, she felt compelled by poverty to at least try. The Depression had only deepened her sense of living on the edge. No wonder her children made up songs ridiculing President Hoover for hoarding turkeys on Thanksgiving...

Holidays! There was another reason to return to Spain. Eladia reminisced about shopping for Christmas presents and fancy dresses, and attending Mass at a real cathedral. Here in America, the family had not had a Christmas tree until 1928—and that was a cottonwood branch festooned with popcorn and painted walnut shells, with a single orange for each child beneath the unlikely tree. Not much had improved in the handful of years since.

Still, something troubled Eladia about her family's social position in a Spanish nation that seemed to be changing for the worse. Her father had been close to the monarchy, but news had reached even the backwater town of Fallon that King Alfonso had fled Spain. She knew from her brother Eduardo, who frequently exchanged letters with their siblings in Spain, that her family was somehow caught up in the transition to Spain's dictator, the man who had driven the King to flee. As Spain descended into more and more political chaos, Eladia wondered whether her mother's offer of a safe harbor would be all that safe.

And what if her oldest children did not wish to return to Spain? Pilar and Trinidad had left school and found jobs. The family could not afford the new busing fee imposed by the school district for high school students, so Jesus was poised to drop out as well. Eladia could not bear the thought of further dividing her family if they could not all make the same decision.

Eladia looked up at the clock over the kitchen table and stiffened her resolve. She stood to pour her cold coffee down the sink just as Marcelino walked through the door with Antonio tagging along beside him. She wasted no time.

"Antonio, go outside and find your brothers. Papa and I need to have a talk."

The nine-year-old looked from one parent to the other and opened his mouth to speak.

"Now," said Eladia coldly.

With Antonio gone from the room, Eladia turned to her husband and gestured for him to sit. She remained standing.

"It is time for things to change around here," she began. "My mother has offered me the opportunity to return to Spain with Eduardo and the children, but—"

"*Ay caramba!* I do not want to go back to Spain!" Marcelino slid onto a chair and leaned it back on the rear two legs as he glared at his wife.

"That is well and good, because she did not invite you. However, I have decided that you have one last chance. I want a house and a ranch that we own, so you will buy one. If you cannot get money from your family or these American businessmen you think are your friends, then I will write to my mother and accept her offer to return to Spain. I will no longer live in America like the paupers who live on the outskirts of Vitoria-Gasteiz." She stopped and waited for a reply.

"How am I to find this money today, as if by magic? I have worked hard all the years we have lived here. Why do you think things are different now?"

Eladia smiled. "Ask your sister and her husband. They own the Grand Hotel in town. They were careful and spent nearly ten years at the Boyer Ranch, working and saving, so they could come to town in style. Ramon has money. He drips of it. Ask your brother-in-law, or I will write to my mother. Either way, your pride will be wounded, but you can decide."

Marcelino let the front of his chair slam back to the floor and he abruptly stood, coming close to Eladia. His hand came up as if he would strike his wife across her face. She did not flinch.

"If you ever try to strike me again, I will be gone on the next train," she said, her voice low and almost humming with tension. "Those are the conditions of my deal. Find the money. Give us a real life. Just know that should you be unable to finally provide a real home, the children and I will leave you."

Marcelino let his hand drop to his side. He sputtered a few swear words in English as he marched out of the kitchen. Eladia heard the front door slam, she presumed behind him. She turned to the sink and began peeling a potato. Pausing for a moment to look back at the table where she had left the letter and telegram, she took a deep breath and exhaled.

***

Eladia smiled as she considered the date she was writing as she signed the quitclaim deed and indenture between her and Marcelino and the Norton and Wood families: June 6, 1931. Seven weeks had passed since she had given her husband the ultimatum. When the documents were recorded, they would be the owners of 178 acres in the Soda Lake District on the west side of Fallon.

Marcelino signed and dated the documents as well, although Eladia observed he was not smiling. No doubt he was wondering how he would repay the loan.

Marcelino's brother-in-law Ramon had agreed to loan them $4,268.75 to buy the ranch. They were to pay him back at the rate of $50 per month, without interest, so Eladia was imagining a celebration in just over seven years. She would be 53 by then, and a landowner.

Eladia was still surprised her husband had pulled it off. A part of her was disappointed, and she'd had difficulty writing the long letter to her mother this morning declining the offer of a return to Spain. But a deal was a deal, and the more news she heard from Spain the more comfortable she was that America was a better place for her children, if not for her. Owning their own ranch would set a different standard of living, she was certain. She spent most of her time at home anyhow, so her dislike of Maine Street, and Fallon, and the English language, would not matter. She had stood her ground.

"I think we should walk across the street to Ramon and Tomasa's hotel and celebrate with a drink at the bar!" she proclaimed as the courthouse clerk let them know they were done with the paperwork.

Marcelino, usually more than happy to spend an hour or two in the bars, looked at his wife with a pained expression, as if she were pouring salt in an open wound. And perhaps she was. But she smiled nonetheless and reached for her purse.

VICTORIA
March 1933
Fallon, Nevada

"What does it mean for the bank to close?" Victoria asked her nervous husband when he returned from town. "Doesn't it close every day? And on Sunday, it is always closed. Your English is not as good as you think. You misunderstood something."

Victor shook his head. This, he told his wife, was not like that—and it was different from earlier runs on the banking system when other banks had closed during the first years of the Depression but somehow the family's money had been safe. This time, President Roosevelt had closed all the banks, including the one with their money. Victor and their son Fabian had just returned from a meeting at which a notable Reno banker tried to convince all the farmers in the valley to relinquish claim to their deposits with his bank, in exchange for a smaller payment from the federal government's Reconstruction Finance Corporation. The ensuing conversation had not been pleasant, Fabian told his mother excitedly.

"At the end of the meeting, old Doc Sawyer stood up and convinced the farmers not to go with that banker from Reno," Fabian said. "You should have seen it!"

Sawyer, a local, had succeeded in convincing the farmers that the bankers, not the depositors, would ultimately benefit from the proposed scheme. Instead, Victor explained, as he took over the narration from Fabian who raced outside to tell his siblings the news, the local farmers agreed to pool what money they could once Roosevelt's "Bank Holiday" had passed and the institutions were reopened. Victor expected to get only 70 cents on the dollar, but it would—eventually—be enough for the bank to sign over the deed to the old Bassett Ranch located south of town in Fallon's Union District. The bank had no use for the property and would be glad to have it off the books. Victor was certain they could move right away and work out the payments later. He had to explain this to Victoria several times before she understood the plan.

"You mean we are moving again?" she asked at last.

"Yes, and we are going to own that ranch," Victor said. "It has a fine adobe house for you. Six rooms and porches all around! There is also a barn, corrals, and plenty of land."

"I do not think I understand."

"*Vitori*, we are finished here. We are done leasing this place. We are going to allow the new bank to take our money as shares, a little bit less than it was worth. But we will still have money. Over time, we will own that ranch. We will never have to move again."

This much Victoria understood.

"I will begin to pack. You get Annie from the yard," she said. A smile spread across her face.

"Where is my father's pocket watch?"

PART FOUR:
Annie
1934–1941

ANNIE
September 1934
Fallon, Nevada

Most people seem to remember their first day of school, but I can't say that I do. The school I went to for the first grade was called "Old High" because it had been the high school previously. My teacher in the first grade was Miss Hilda Swenson. She was very picky about her students keeping their desks neat and I had a lot of trouble with that.

My best friend, Louise, sat right in front of me in class. Louise was very neat, and I remember one day we were supposed to be organizing these little cards with the letters of the alphabet printed on them.

"Annie, your cards are not in the right order," Louise said when she turned around to see how I was doing. "Look how neat mine are."

I didn't say a word. I just got out of my desk and messed up all of Louise's cards, pushing a few of them onto the floor. Miss Swenson was not happy with me, but thankfully Louise stayed my friend.

Louise and I were friends because she lived about a mile from us with her grandparents, and we rode the school bus together. My family had moved to the Bassett Ranch in Union District in 1933 and we lived there when I started first grade. The Bassett Ranch, probably homesteaded by Elmer E. Bassett, was old and once had been quite large. Highway 50, the old Lincoln Highway which went clear across the United States, cut through the property at the time we moved there. All that remained of the Bassett place in 1933 was a short 60 acres. But it was the only place my parents had ever owned, in all their years in the United States.

Even though I was happy at home and found ways to have fun, I was glad to go to school. At home, I had only imaginary playmates and my parents. I remember Pop as having a lot of time to spend with me. Sometimes he used to watch the cows while they pastured the ditches or grain stubble, to keep them from getting into the alfalfa. I always tagged along, and we spent the time playing games, especially cards. I remember we took imaginary trips to Spain, where he had been born, and he would tell me about the Old Country and the things he had done there. He had lived in the town of Ea, right on the ocean, and was an excellent swimmer. He said the tourists would throw coins into the water and he and any other boys who were around would dive for them. On our imaginary trips to Spain, we would "visit" the Rubianes relatives he had left behind, so I knew all their names and life stories.There was a fairly large orchard near the house on the Bassett place. I remember a lot of plum trees, a big apple tree and a pear tree, and lots of yellow rose bushes of the half-wild variety. In the summertime, we would sit in the shade of the orchard and play Casino and Fish and other card games the names of which I have long ago forgotten. It seemed like we had it easy. I suppose this is one of the advantages of having older parents. My mother was 40 and my father was 42 when I was born. By the time I entered school, most of the other children in the family were gone from home and were self-supporting. My sister Jessie was a senior in high school when I started first grade, and she made all my clothes that year. Mom bought the sewing material and Jessie made several dresses for me to wear. She didn't use a pattern but cut them out by using another dress to go by.

The house we lived in at the Bassett Ranch was made of adobe. It was rectangular in shape with six rooms. Because there was no hallway, every room had at least three doors opening into other rooms or the outside. There were two screened porches, one on the east and one on the south side of the house. They were covered with Virginia creepers. I liked those creepers when they were leafed out; they seemed to make it cooler, and the house looked nicer with them.

I guess the stores in Fallon did not have many paint selections in those days, or if they did it was too expensive for us. When we painted, we used Kalsomine, which was a water-based paint and not particularly good. I painted my room, my dresser, and my storage trunk blue—all the same shade. I thought it was quite beautiful.

We had no running water in the house. There was a hand pump on the porch where we pumped cold water. Hot water had to be heated in a pan on the wood-burning kitchen stove. We took baths in a round washtub set in the middle of the kitchen, after heating the water on the stove. I was really surprised when the Ernst family moved across the road from the Bassett Ranch and fixed their house with hot and cold running water and a bathroom. I didn't understand the mysteries of how it all worked, but I was impressed!

ANNIE

December 1936

Fallon, Nevada

I was in my bed one night, about two weeks before Christmas, pretending to be asleep but secretly eavesdropping on Mom and my sister, Jessie, who were talking in the living room. Because the Bassett house had all those doors connecting room to room, secrets were hard to keep.

"I bought some things for Annie to put in her stocking," Jessie was saying. "We can tell her they're from Santa Claus." "Santa Claus?" asked Mom. "He comes to your house, not just to the party in town?"

Jessie and Mom were speaking Basque, as we always did at home—particularly with my mother, whose English was not good.

Jessie tried to explain the difference between the American Santa Claus and Spain's traditions at Christmastime. Mom didn't really understand, but she finally agreed that it would be nice for me to have some presents at home. I was shocked. The stocking I hung up each year was one of my brown cotton stockings that I wore all the time. I had learned about Santa Claus at school, and the news that he was just my sister came as a blow. I knew enough not to tell them that I had overheard their conversation, because if I did, it would probably be the end of Santa Claus and presents for good.

My brother Tony had gotten married just a few months before to a wonderful lady named Van. Because I was so much younger than my siblings, she was something like a second mother to me. The day after the eavesdropping incident, Tony and Van arrived with a Christmas tree. Was I ever thrilled! Van said her family always had a tree, and I guess my siblings had them when they lived in Kingston, but we had never had one at the Bassett house.

Van also gave me a little bit of money when she and Tony brought the tree, and I was excited to get to do some shopping with her in town. I bought a comb for Tony and a handkerchief each for

Mom and Van, and then I was out of money. With tears in my eyes, I asked Van what I was going to do about Pop.

"You need to learn the value of money," she said. "You should have stuck to your budget."

I didn't know what a budget was, but when we got home, I came up with my own solution. I went through the family pictures and found a snapshot of myself taken at my First Communion. I put it in an envelope and put that under the tree for my father.

When Christmas morning came, I gave my best performance of acting surprised at what I found in my stocking. I can only remember one of the things I got: a blue metal bank shaped like a little bucket with a handle. It had a blue and white flower design on it. I really loved that bank, especially with my newfound interest in money! I know there were a couple of other things, but I don't remember what they were. I also remember Pop said how pleased he was with that photograph of me. I wasn't the only actor in the family, I guess.

Tony had arrived at our house with a wrapped package which he put under the Christmas tree. It was labeled "To me from me." He was laughing and joking about it. When we opened presents, it turned out to be a pair of gloves, which he needed for work, and he thought that probably would be the only way he would get them.

For dinner that night, Van had invited us to their place in Stillwater, one of the rural districts outside the town of Fallon. My folks drove us down there in our 1929 Chevy. It sure seemed like a long way. Van gave me another present, a book called *The Three Billy Goats Gruff*. It was the first book I ever owned. Over and over, I read about those goats, and the troll who lived under the bridge. The story is about not being too greedy, and I guess our simple Christmas—and my father's joy at receiving something he already owned—goes well with that moral.

We celebrated long into the night with Tony and Van. Mom and Pop had paid off the bank note on the Bassett Ranch and wanted to enjoy themselves. Our place was now the Rubianes Ranch!

ANNIE
June 1938
Winnemucca, Nevada

The train ride from Hazen to Winnemucca was the most exciting thing that had happened to me in my ten years of simple living. I have no idea how my mother was able to leave the ranch, because she never seemed to go anywhere. She just stayed home and worked. But right after my birthday, she told me we were going to Winnemucca to visit my sisters, and that I could stay there for a while once she came home. Mom did not drive, and Pop could not go because of the farm, so the train was our only option.

Tony and Van took us to Hazen, about 20 miles away, to catch the train. The seats seemed very plush with their soft padding and lovely gray fabric. The train made a lot of noise, but I didn't mind a bit. Those fancy gray seats and the sense of adventure made my trip very enjoyable.

While Mom was in Winnemucca, we stayed at the Winnemucca Hotel where my sister Polly had worked as a waitress when she first moved to Winnemucca a few years back. Polly was now married to George Etchart, and they had a little house. My other sister, Jessie, was married to Eddie Heinz and they were living at our cousin Modesto's house. His mother was our dad's sister, and they lived in Spain some of the time and America the rest. Modesto's son, Juan, is just a couple years younger than I am, so we spent some time goofing off without the adults. In the evenings, Jessie and Eddie would take us to an ice cream parlor at Eagle Drug on the main street and drink Coca-Cola. Their favorite was Cherry Coke. The person who worked behind the counter was called a "soda jerk." He would put a charge of cherry syrup in a glass and then fill it up with Coke. *Mmm.* I had only water and coffee to drink at home, so these sodas were high living for me!

When Mom went back to Fallon, I moved to Polly and George's house. George was working out of town and only came home on weekends. Polly would do her housework and gardening in the morning and then after lunch we would get dressed up and go visiting. George's sister Grace lived just a few blocks away, and we went there quite often. Her daughter Blanche was several years younger than I, but we had fun together.

One morning when I woke up, I came into Polly's kitchen and found this pink and yellow thing sitting on my plate.

"What's that?" I asked.

"It's a grapefruit, silly."

I had never even seen a grapefruit before and wasn't too sure about eating it. I tasted a little bit and made a face at how sour it was.

"You won't get to go to the swimming pool if you don't eat it all," said my sister. It was gone in a flash!

That day, instead of going visiting, Polly and I went to the municipal swimming pool. We didn't go swimming; we just went to the pool to be social. Polly had no interest in getting into water that came above her ankles, and I didn't own a swimming suit, but we sat on the benches under the shade trees and watched everyone else swim.

Jessie taught me to crochet that summer. Whenever she came to Polly's house, we would have a lesson. I wasn't a particularly good pupil, although I did finish a rather elaborate doily. It had to be starched with sugar water and shaped around several water glasses until it dried. When it came time to leave, I packed the doily in my little bag and waited for Jessie and Eddie to pick me up. They had the weekend off and were able to make the drive to Fallon. I was soon home.

Mom and Pop asked to hear all about my summer of fun, so for the next few nights we sat together in one of the screened porches on our house and I regaled them with stories.

"Jessie and Eddie even took me to the movies!" I told my folks, who had never seen a motion picture in their lives. "It was a scary movie, too! I spent the night with Jessie and Eddie after the movie and . . ."

My voice trailed off.

"What is it, Annie?" asked Pop.

I hesitated and then explained what had happened. After the scary picture show, we came home and went to bed as usual—me on the couch in the front room—but I couldn't sleep because I was afraid. Eddie's clothes were draped over a chair in the front room, and because of the way they were draped (and because my imagination was working overtime) it looked like a man in dark pants and a white shirt sitting there. I was so sure it was a person that I finally started to cry and called for Jessie. She got up and consoled me and moved the clothes to show me what they were, and I finally went to sleep.

Both my folks smiled at this story.

"You should not be afraid, Annie," said my father.

I looked at my mother and she was nodding. This seemed funny to me, because Mom was so superstitious, she seemed afraid of everything."You can read, write, and speak English," Mom said. "You can get along anywhere. Your Pop and I can't do those things as well as you, but we came to this country when we were young, and—look—we made it fine! Do I need to tell you the story of the girl with the chestnut hair and the boat ride to America again?" Mom smiled and tipped her head to one side.

"And do I need to tell you about being a buckaroo living on my own instead of going to high school?" added my father.

I remember thinking that Mom was right. She couldn't read or write English, and her speaking was sometimes backward, but she managed to do a lot of things well. Pop had overcome a lot, too. I was going to be fine. From that day forward, I was rarely scared of life, and I dreamed some big dreams.

ANNIE
June 1939
Fallon, Nevada

One morning, I was lollygagging in my room, reading a book from the school library, when I heard a clanging sound outside. The clanging meant Mom was nearby. I was up from the bed like a shot and raced into the kitchen. It was my job to have breakfast fixed when the folks got home from doing their morning chores. I was late!

My mother helped my dad milk cows every morning and night—by hand of course. No machines for a small operation like ours! We had about ten cows. Immediately after milking, the cream was separated from the whole milk by a machine called a "cream separator" which was turned by hand. There was a large round bowl that was placed at the top of the cream separator, and beneath it there was a system of curved metal disks. The whole milk was put into the round bowl. Ours was quite large and must have held between two and three gallons of milk. My father would then turn the handle on the machine and the milk filtered through the disks. It had to be turned at a fast pace until all the milk had been put through. I don't know how long this took, but it must have been 20 or 30 minutes. As the milk went through the disks, the cream was separated and came out one spigot while the skimmed milk came out another. This milk was then fed to the pigs we raised.

When the bowl and disks had to be taken to the house to be washed, my mother was the one who carried them. Our house was about one-eighth of a mile across the highway from the barn. Because the bowl was so large and awkward to handle, Mom carried it on her head, something she'd learned to do as a little girl in Spain. The load was heavy because all the disks were carried in that bowl, as well as the large milk strainer, but she balanced it all on her head and carried the bucket of cream in one hand. She carried this big load from the house to the barn, and then back again, every morning and every evening, every day of the week. Tourists driving along Highway 50 often slowed down to look as they went by, and at least one time I remember some people stopped and asked if they could take her picture.

"Annie?"

Mom was calling for me and I hadn't had time to get the potatoes in the skillet. Every morning I cooked a big cast iron frying pan full of potatoes. I peeled, diced, and fried them. When Mom and Pop came in, I would add some scrambled eggs to the potatoes and cook them until the eggs were set up, and that was breakfast. We all three drank coffee with lots of sugar and milk in it.

"Annie!"

Mom sounded impatient.

"Bring a cup and come get some of this cream."

This was a good sign. Every morning, the cream was put into a five-gallon milk can which was kept in the cool cellar. The "cream man" came to all the ranches and picked up everyone's cream and took it to the Fallon Creamery, where it was made into butter and cheese. The Fallon Creamery was on the west side of North Maine Street, in the first building just north of the railroad tracks. Many of the farmers in Fallon milked cows and sold the cream, and that was usually a big part of their livelihood. It provided us with a regular check every month.

Very rarely, Mom would use a cup of the cream and whip it for use on some sort of dessert, usually Jell-O or rice pudding. This didn't happen very often because the sale of that cream represented our income. It seemed like this was going to be a lucky day, but here I was behind with my one chore! I expected to get in trouble. I could already imagine that Jell-O with whipped cream disappearing before my eyes!

"Coming, Mom!"

Breakfast was late, and I did get a scolding, but we still had dessert that night. My parents were in a good mood because they had a little extra money that month and Pop could hire a man to help put up the hay. After dinner, the three of us piled into the Chevy and drove into town. Pop parked in front of the Owl Club on Maine Street, and Mom and I sat in the car watching people go by. This was high entertainment for us country folk, but for my dad it was an important task.

When it was time for haying season to start, transient workers would come to Fallon for jobs. They hitchhiked or rode the rails. We called them "hobos," and they lived in a shady, tree-covered area called Hobo Jungle, down by the Kent Company's alfalfa mill.

After a few minutes of sizing up the potential workers who were walking up and down the street, my dad walked over to one and struck up a conversation. He was looking for a man who could handle a team of horses because we did not have a tractor. Hay was piled on wagons that had a net, made with cable and a board frame, laid across the wagon bed. A team of two horses pulled the wagons into the stackyard, where Pop and the hired man would use a system of cables and pulleys to stack the hay.

"We are lucky today!" Pop announced as he brought the man back to the car. Apparently, the man had recently returned from Mexico where he spent the winter, but he had hay-stacking experience from the prior summer spent in Winnemucca. Mom felt that since she and Pop had originally met in Winnemucca when they were young, this was a good sign. Mom loved to find "signs" to help her make decisions. Pop only cared if the man could work.

Pop explained the conditions of hire.

"You sleep with the grain," he began, meaning the granary, a word he didn't know in English. "I pay one dollar a day, two if you work the stack, and we give you breakfast, lunch, and supper."

This must have sounded good to the man, whose name I can't remember, because he jumped in the car with us, and we drove to Hobo Jungle to collect his bedroll and clothes. On the way back to the ranch, he told stories about his time in Mexico. I was enthralled by the idea of travel, and his stories were the perfect end to a good day that had started with me worried about getting in trouble. I felt so good, I told him we had some Jell-O left at home.

I think he was as happy about that as I was.

ANNIE
August 1940
Fallon, Nevada

"I am going to start calling you Speed."

My brother Fabian, who had taken up the name Bob because Americans couldn't say his real name, was sitting with Mom in the living room of our house, having a glass of lemonade, when I ran past them on my way to the kitchen.

Mom laughed at Bob's jest. "Annie is always in a hurry," she said.

I sauntered back into the living room with an apple, taking it as slowly as I could to make a point. Bob loved to tease. He was always so full of life. He had been working throughout the Depression on various jobs—from ranching down in Stillwater District to laying cement for ditches with the Civilian Conservation Corps, one of President Roosevelt's relief agencies, better known as the CCC. My father had suffered a ruptured appendix in June, so Bob had come to live with us to take care of the ranch while Pop recovered. I really enjoyed having him around, even if he did saddle me with a nickname.

Names were a funny thing in my family. My brothers and sisters had all slowly but surely Americanized their names over time. Tony got the nickname Tip from someone, and during his time with the CCC, Bob's friends started calling him Cotton because they said he could soak up so much beer. My mother didn't like that name very much. She didn't even like calling her son Bob, and always called him Fabian or *Fabianchu*, which in Basque means "little Fabian." Jessie was often called "Babe," because for the eleven years before I came along, she was the baby of the family. I don't remember Polly having a nickname, but thanks to Bob, I became Speed to everyone.

When I started seventh grade a few weeks later, I went out for the track team. I was skinny as a beanpole and, Mom was right,

I loved to run. I made the team and soon everyone at school started calling me Speed, just like my family.

When I wasn't running track that year, I was learning about the expectations of domestic life. Girls were required to take Home Economics, while the boys took Manual Training, or "Shop." I was attending seventh grade at Oats Park School. The regular classrooms were upstairs, but Home Economics and Manual Training were taught in the basement. I never saw the boys' half of the basement, but our half had big sinks, long tables, gas stoves, a refrigerator or two, and an entire room filled with sewing machines and tall benches. Miss Alice Wade was our teacher. The first thing we had to learn was how to sew a straight seam, and then we learned to make flat-felled seams. I hated flat-felled seams so, of course, mine never turned out well. My friend Bonnie and I had Home Economics together. When Miss Wade told us that we would be making a pair of slacks and a blouse, Bonnie said, "Let's make matching outfits." I thought that sounded great and we had a third friend, Elenor, who decided to go along with this plan too. We picked out the material at J.C. Penney—navy blue for the slacks, and red, white, and blue stripes for the top. Miss Wade said we should wash the material, first in hot water and then in cold water, to shrink it before we began sewing. That way, she said, the garment would not shrink when we were finished. We were to wash the material at home. Bonnie said this was not necessary; she said you just cut a piece of material five inches square, swished it around under the faucet (or in my case, the hand pump), dried it, and then measured it. If the swatch was still five inches square, you were okay.

I didn't know any different, so I followed Bonnie's instructions and my fabric passed the test, so we laboriously made our outfits. We were so proud of them. The blouses had long sleeves, straight with no cuffs or gathers. We put them on as soon as they were finished, but after wearing them a couple times, we had to wash them. Guess what? My slacks came through fine, but the blouse had shrunk. It wasn't as long, and the sleeves didn't reach to my wrists anymore. I asked why mine was the only one that had shrunk, and Bonnie and Elenor admitted that their mothers had insisted they preshrink their material according to Miss Wade's directions. No one had told me, so I had the ill-fitting blouse. My mother didn't see too much wrong with it, and she had spent good money for the material, so I had to keep wearing it.

We also took cooking lessons that year. We learned to make cinnamon toast. As usual, I had never even heard of it, so I thought it was fabulous. It tasted good with my morning coffee. We also learned to make hot milk sponge cake. You beat some eggs until they were light and fluffy, then you added sugar and salt and one cup of boiling hot milk with some oil stirred in. Finish up with some flour and, if we had it, some baking powder. When I told my mother about this, she said I could make it at home. She and my dad liked it. It was a lot better than no cake at all, so I made it every chance I could get. I would get it all mixed and put into the pans. Mom took care of firing up the wood-burning stove. After a while, she would put her hand in the oven and say, "That feels just right." I would then put the cake in to bake. I guess it *was* "just right," because it always came out fine.

Even with Bob around the house that summer and fall, I was still raised a lot like an only child. From the time I was nine or ten, I'd had a whole group of imaginary fiends. My name in this imaginary group was LaRue Davies, and my boyfriend, who in my mind's eye had red hair, was named Bill Barnett. I don't know where I got these names, but I found magazine pictures to show what we looked like. Somewhere along the way, I had started to write short stories about us, including one called "The Red Cross Girls in Arabia." LaRue Davies and three others from my imaginary group were the Red Cross girls. I had plans to write a whole series of short stories about them but, alas, the track team came along, and I guess I was just going too fast.

ANNIE
December 1941
Fallon, Nevada

I was out riding my bike on the afternoon of Sunday, December 7th. One of my friends and I had taken a long ride around the countryside to while away a lazy afternoon. When I came home toward evening, I found my parents and Bob gathered around the radio in our living room. They told me about the bombing of Pearl Harbor, but no one knew much at that point. I went to bed with more questions than answers.

Monday was a school day, and although my parents discussed keeping me home, I wanted to be with my friends, so I boarded the school bus as usual. When my friend Jeneece Weaver got on the bus, she told me her cousin, Dick, had been on the USS *Arizona*, one of the ships bombed at Pearl Harbor. Jeneece did not know what had happened to her cousin, but she was pretty shaken. Everyone was. Our country had been attacked and we were feeling both patriotic and afraid. Not much schoolwork got done that day.

When I returned home from school, Tony and Van were there. They were sitting with my parents and Bob, and once again everyone was listening to the radio.

"What will happen now?" my mother asked. I could see she was nervous and wanted someone to reassure her. Her English was not good enough to understand the news story we'd just heard informing the nation that the President had already signed the declaration of war with Japan that afternoon.

"War."

Pop looked mad as he said the word, which seemed to hang in the air for several seconds. Tony and Bob jumped in, trying to out-do one another with their brave talk of going to fight.

Mom was having nothing to do with that.

"It does not matter to us," she insisted.

"Mom, people from Fallon may already be dead," Tony insisted. "Ray Weaver came into the store several times today. His son was at Pearl Harbor, and they are afraid they will get bad news."

Tony was working at Sewell's Store, and he seemed to know everyone in town, including Ray Weaver, the local postmaster.

"It's true, Mom," I added. "Jeneece told me about it on the bus."

"See? We have to fight back," Tony declared. "The Weavers are our friends."

"Nobody in this family did any fighting in the last war," Mom said, her voice ringing with a tone of authority, as if she was coaxing us to agree with her and therefore make everything better.

My father sighed.

"I was not an American citizen then. I am now. And the boys . . ." His voice trailed off.

PART FIVE:
War and Peace
1942–1948

ELADIA
Fallon, Nevada
March 1942

"Candidate Erquiaga, have you performed any service to support the war effort?"

Seated in the back of the courtroom where Judge Ben Curler was questioning her son, Eladia could not understand the man's English words.

"*Qué?*" she asked her husband, a bit too loudly for a courtroom.

Marcelino whispered the Spanish translation and the two returned their attention to their son and the judge.

"No, sir," said Jesus in a nervous voice, high-pitched and with a hint of impatience. "All I have done is try to enlist in either the Navy or the Marine Corps, but they wouldn't have me because I'm not a citizen."

Judge Curler frowned.

"Son, do you want to enlist?"

Jesus cleared his throat. "Yes, sir. I tried to get a job working on the ALCAN Highway to Alaska, but there was some kind of mix-up and the Employment Board turned me in for not being a citizen and trying to work. I don't know what I'm supposed to do if I can't work and I can't enlist, sir. Do you?"

"*Qué?*"

Marcelino shushed his wife. He beamed with pride as he quietly translated for her his son's statement to the judge. She understood his smile at once. The family had come to witness today's proceeding because they were angry at how Jesus, who had lived in America since he was four years old, had been treated by the bureaucrat at the Employment Board. Marcelino himself had finally become an American citizen in 1939, and Eladia agreed with him that their son and three eldest daughters, who were also born in Spain and were now productive working members of society, deserved better treatment.

Pilar had married another Basque, Tony Ormachea, and the young couple lived near Susanville, California, with two sons. Trinidad, who had made her name as American as she could by shortening it to Trini, lived in Reno and worked at J.C. Penney, while Maria Luisa—"Mary" to everyone these days—had married Reynold "Doc" Clifford and was expecting her first child in a couple months. Mary and Doc lived in Tonopah.

Marcelino and Eladia took pride in the success of all their children, no matter where they had been born or where they were on their journey to citizenship or careers. Jose Luis and Carmen were still in school, but their son Antonio—Tony to his American friends—was away at college in Utah. This was a first for any Erquiaga that Marcelino could remember, in any country. Tony's future looked bright. But Jesus needed work, and Eladia understood enough of what was happening to hope the judge would do the right thing.She got her wish.

"Son, I think that's very commendable, and I'm going to help you out today," said Judge Curler. "I'm going to approve your candidacy for citizenship in this great country, on the condition you change your name to Joseph. This Jesus business . . ."

The judge pronounced the name in English, which, without a Spanish pronunciation, did sound out of place in the day's proceedings."Well, that's just a mouthful, son," the judge continued. "But you will make a fine American and, I suspect, a fine soldier. Enlist as fast as you can. The Nazis and Japs won't wait."

The judge banged his gavel as if to punctuate his announcement and directed the clerk to summon the next candidate for citizenship.

"*Qué dice?*" asked Eladia impatiently, pulling on Marcelino's shirt sleeve.

"He said Jesus can go to war and fight for America!" exclaimed Marcelino in English. "*Jesus es Americano!*"

The judge banged his gravel once more to quiet the resulting outburst of laughter.***

With Jesus—now calling himself "Joe"—taken care of and summer coming to the Lahontan Valley, Eladia threw herself into work at the Soda Lake Ranch.

She had developed a knack for gardening, and her vegetables were already yielding the food she would need for Marcelino, herself, and the two children still at home, as well as for Joe during whatever time he had left before the military called him up. Tony had returned home from college in June, and by that time Eladia had a wood-burning stove set out in the yard under some cottonwood trees so it would be cooler to do her work. She took to canning tomatoes and string beans and made plans for canning apricots when the trees in the small orchard behind the house provided fruit. She told Marcelino she wanted even more garden space, so he diverted water from the irrigation ditch and plowed another spot nearby.

The garden drew jackrabbits in from the dessert, and a worried Eladia informed her husband and sons that they would have to shoot the vermin at night to keep her crops safe. Her garden was the first project that had inspired her in some years. The men were happy to oblige, eager for the target practice so that when deer hunting season came, they would be ready.

Within a matter of weeks, Joe received word he had been drafted, and his parents were at the train station in Hazen, seeing him off to Reno on his way to Sacramento and service in the Army. Eladia insisted Marcelino drive her to church on the way home so she could light a candle. Then she returned to the stove under the cottonwood trees, thankful for the distraction and trying to consider what the war might mean for her sons. She understood it was possible Tony could be drafted as well, despite his college success, and while she had no love for the Americans' war, she had heard enough from her siblings about Francoist Spain to have a dislike of Fascism. Not for the first time, she congratulated herself for convincing Marcelino to buy the Soda Lake Ranch. Spain had ceased to hold any interest for her. Tomatoes, zucchini, and apricots had taken its place in her heart.

VICTORIA
Fallon, Nevada
September 1942

Victoria clutched her father's broken pocket watch in one hand and her rosary in the other. She was seated at the back of St. Patrick's Church, Victor at her side. The church was empty except for the two of them. They had stopped by to light a candle and say a few prayers after a shopping trip in town. Victoria's lips moved in silent prayer. Victor dozed in and out of consciousness, somehow managing not to snore.

The first prayer Victoria said was for the safety of her son, Fabian, whom everyone else had taken to calling Bob. He had been drafted—a word and process Victoria did not understand—within just a few weeks of the attack on Pearl Harbor. After traveling by train to Salt Lake City, he had enlisted in the Army and been stationed at various military bases around the country for training in something called a "tank" with the Fourth Armored Division. Victoria lived with the daily fear he would be shipped overseas to fight.

Her second prayer was for her son Antonio. Tony had also been drafted, but when he reported for his physical, his long history of ulcers and a back injury sustained when he was thrown from a horse in 1936 precluded him from service. While Victoria was relieved the military did not want her oldest son, Tony had fallen into a depression and seemed angry that he could not "do his part."

Victoria shuddered at the memory of the day a despondent and angry Tony came to the house for dinner. Ray Weaver had been to Sewell's Store again, this time with the news his son had been declared dead. He was in a watery grave with the rest of the crew of the USS *Arizona* in Pearl Harbor. But before the Navy had certified this fact, the boy's mother had suffered the heartbreak of having the Christmas card she'd mailed her son be returned, marked "Undeliverable," and she subsequently had been required to visit burn hospitals in California to search for her son. The Navy had worried, and the Weavers had somehow held out a terrible hope, that Dick Weaver had lived, burned beyond recognition to anyone but a mother, and could not speak to identify himself. The fact that this implied perhaps there were patients from Pearl Harbor fitting that description terrified Victoria even more.

"You can fight on the home front," Victor had assured his son, parroting the words of President Roosevelt, whose radio addresses kept Victor attentive to any news about the war. "Maybe you can help sell war bonds. The President says they are important." Victor's tone implied the President might have given him this advice in person, they were so close, but Tony remained disappointed.

Finally, Victoria prayed that the war would not claim her sons-in-law. Daughter Polly and her husband, George Etchart, lived and worked at a mine in Golconda, outside Winnemucca, and George had not yet been drafted. Jessie was living at Fluorspar Mine near Fallon. Her husband, Eddie Heinz, had not been drafted either, or this suited Victoria just fine.

Her prayers finished, Victoria reached for her purse and stored her rosary and pocket watch. She elbowed Victor in the ribs to rouse him from his slumber.

"Vic!" she whispered. "Let's go! Annie will be done with school now. Time to pick her up and go home."

Victor rubbed the sleep from his eyes, made the sign of the cross as if he had been deep in prayer himself, and stood to go.

"We are going to the ballpark when we get Annie," he announced.

Victoria rolled her eyes. Ever since Victor had won twenty gallons of gasoline in a promotional drawing sponsored the Fallon Garage, he and Annie had made regular trips to the ball field at Oats Park to watch the young men play.

"They will all have to go to war soon," Victor explained. "We should let them know we support them while the games and the free gasoline last."

Victoria thought of the growing use of ration stamps for gasoline, sugar, and other staples. She feared this would get worse, and the idea of Victor using extra fuel to drive to these baseball games irked her. She made a mental note to pray about rationing, and her husband's tendency to waste things, on her next trip to church.

"Let's go! Annie will be waiting."

***

Victoria was glad to have work to keep her mind off the war—and raising turkeys for slaughter was certainly work. As she placed the brightly colored marbles in the turkey mash, a tactic she had learned long ago to encourage the dumb birds to peck at their food, she reflected on farm life. It was never easy, but the honest labor was good for the soul. There were the daily milking chores. She helped Victor with the haying if they had no hired hand (men had become increasingly hard to find as the war effort took over every aspect of life). And she had her turkeys.

Each spring she would buy about 50 turkey chicks and raise them in the brooder, a warming room with a heating lamp overhead. She spent her time caring for the little black birds, keeping their water clean with potassium permanganate, and ensuring no skunks made their way into the shed where the turkeys were kept. It took time and energy. More than once, while trying to protect her cash crop, Victoria had experienced the spray of a skunk intent on stealing a turkey. But they needed the money more than she needed clean clothes.

This weekend, a husband-and-wife team would come to the Rubianes farm from town to help butcher the birds. Victoria had prepared the weights to hang from the turkey's mouths once they were hung by their feet. The exercise reminded her of the boys hanging from geese at home in Lekeitio. There was nothing festive about butchering turkeys, and certainly not about the nasty birds themselves. Victoria would enjoy though, just a little, watching the man from town stab the birds in the neck so they could bleed out, while she and the man's wife quickly pulled off the feathers and washed the carcasses. The work was hard, and somewhat vile, but it served as both a distraction from her worries and an outlet for her pent-up frustrations.

Moving from the turkeys' shed to the small storage building next door, Victoria checked to be sure she had enough paper on hand to wrap the birds for transport to Kent's warehouse in town, from where they would be shipped to market. She smiled at the thought of the payment she and Victor would receive. The money would see them through the winter, she hoped. Then she thought of Fabian and wondered what the winter would bring for him. Angry and fretting, she slammed the door to the storage building. It was time to kill some turkeys.

ANNIE
February 1943
Fallon, Nevada

Jeneece Weaver and I waited in the high school auditorium, which we called "The Pit" because it was a sunken space in the middle of the building, for over an hour. We were eager to see the award Churchill County High School was receiving from the United States War Department. Everyone was keyed up and excited—all for an award about how much scrap metal we had collected over the school year.

Since the beginning of the war, scrap iron drives went on all the time. They were important because the country needed all the iron it could get to make guns and other tools of war. When Fallon held these drives, we were let out of school for the day to collect scrap. The high school sponsored contests between the classes, and we were all feeling patriotic and eager to help, so we didn't take advantage of the situation for personal fun. There may have been an occasional student who took off and went fishing, but very few. Jeneece and I joined up with her cousin, who had a pickup, and we would go around to the various farms in Lahontan Valley. A lot of farmers donated old machinery or tools they no longer used. We would load it up and haul it off to a central location where it was sent away to be melted down and used to make something for the war effort.

Apparently, we had been quite successful. Our school had collected the most scrap iron in the entire state of Nevada. The prize was a commemorative brick taken from Independence Hall in Philadelphia. Independence Hall originally had been built with bricks brought over from England before the Revolutionary War. The Hall had been repaired in the late thirties, and some of the original bricks were taken out. One had been presented to each state sometime after the war began, and Nevada's brick had been sent to Fallon for the ceremony. I guess the connection was meant to symbolize that Independence Hall represented the colonies winning their freedom from England, and the scrap iron drives were part of the fight to preserve that freedom in the war with Germany and Japan.

The ceremony turned out to be shorter than we expected, but it was still exciting. When it was over, we hitched a ride with two boys neither of us knew very well and we drove up and down Maine Street—what we called "dragging Maine." Only three or four kids in my class even had a car. We typically walked downtown from school during the lunch hour while the kids who did have cars would drag Maine. Sometimes one of them would stop to ask if we wanted a ride, and we thought that was great. The boy I had a crush on, whom my friends and I called by the code name "Timber Wolf," had a car and sometimes would give me a ride. That was always a real thrill because he was a senior. On those nights, a lot of sighs and giggles were exchanged on the telephone between my girlfriends and me.When we passed the Fallon Foxhole, Jeneece piped up from the boys' car.

"Hey! Let's stop for a soda and a game of pool," she suggested, and the guys were quick to oblige.

The Fallon Foxhole, a teenage recreation center sponsored by the Rotary Club, had opened just after Christmas 1942. I didn't get to go there very often, because my folks had stopped taking me to town for recreation as the war drug on. The Foxhole had ping-pong tables, shuffleboard, a juke box for music to dance to, and various other things. I was excited to go inside—especially with a boy or two—but I was also secretly hoping that Timber Wolf wouldn't find out!

ELADIA
March 1944
Fallon, Nevada

The letters from her sons arrived on the same day. Because both were written in English so the military censors could review them for any classified information, Eladia waited for her daughter, Carmen, to come home from school and translate them into Spanish. She did not trust Marcelino's English, and she worried he might leave out any bad news. She was also suspicious that something had been blacked out on the letter from Joe.

When Carmen got home, Eladia handed her the letters and they sat at the kitchen table.

"Joe says he left Africa, but the name of the city or wherever he is now has been blacked out," Carmen said. Her Spanish, to Eladia's ear, was tainted with the hint of an American accent. While her younger American-born children were still fluent in their parents' native tongue, Eladia could always hear a difference from the way their Spanish-born siblings spoke.

"Why is something missing?"

"The Army does that, Mama. It's nothing to worry about. I heard on the news that the Allies are fighting in Italy, so maybe he moved there."

Eladia pursed her lips and folded her hands neatly in her lap, rubbing the soft cotton material of the apron she always wore over her dresses. She was not interested in Carmen's guesswork about the war. Her daughter might be a senior in high school, but she was still a child in Eladia's eyes.

"He also says they all had dysentery, and there were flies everywhere, but not much else. He sounds fine to me. He sends his love."

Eladia was unsure that dysentery sounded "fine," but she nodded and handed over the letter from her other son, Antonio.

He had been fortunate from the beginning of his time in the Navy. Although drafted and forced to leave college after only a year and a half, he possessed enough education to be sent for special training at the West Coast Sound School in San Diego. After some time on the USS *Rathburne*, he remained stationed in Southern California. Once, when home on leave, he had tried to explain something called "sonar" to his parents, but Eladia did not understand the concept. She only knew he was not fighting, was instead some kind of instructor, and for that she was grateful.

"Tony says he has a lot of friends at the base," Carmen added, eliciting a flinch when her mother heard the easy way Carmen changed Antonio's name to fit their American life. *No judge had changed his name*, Eladia thought.

"He says that they all drink too much, but he wants you to know he doesn't drink, Mama."

Eladia and Carmen exchanged glances. Alcohol was a tense subject in their home. Eladia nodded and Carmen continued.

"He says Ken Calvert, his friend from college, is stationed in the same city as he is, so they are able to spend time together."

Carmen paused. "Imagine—they were in Utah for school and then they meet up in California in the service. That's what they call a 'small world,' Mama." She had a smile on her face, but Eladia did not return it.

Before either of them could say another word, young Paul Ormachea walked in from outside and plopped himself on the floor.

At age five, the oldest grandson in the Erquiaga family was spending a few weeks with his grandparents, while his parents remained in Susanville with his two younger brothers. He was fluent in Spanish and began chattering at his grandmother and aunt, saying he was tired of playing outside and he was hungry. He also asked about his uncles, neither of whom he had met.

"I am going to war soon, too, Grandma," he announced, puffing out his chest with pride.

Carmen shushed her nephew. "Don't talk like that! You are too little to think about fighting. You can barely help Grandpa trap the gophers in the field," she teased.

The ranch land in Soda Lake District consisted mostly of sand, but gophers found ways to burrow into ditch banks and caused all kinds of trouble. The local irrigation district offered a bounty for trapping the nuisance rodents, and Marcelino had made gopher trapping a hobby. A few extra dollars from the bounty now and then didn't hurt either.

During the Depression, Marcelino and Eladia had been forced to give up a few acres of their small ranch because they could not pay the taxes. But with all the children except Carmen out of the house and on their own, it was easier to make ends meet. The Erquiagas' youngest son, Jose Luis, had been granted an agricultural deferment when his brothers were both drafted. For a time, he had stayed with his parents to help with the ranch, but now he spent as much time in Susanville with his sister and her husband, helping them as well. He brought Paul back and forth on his trips, and he was currently away.

"Speaking of your grandfather, I need to go help him feed the cows," said Carmen. "Paul, you stay with Grandma."

"Can we have *café con leche*?" Paul asked, his voice pleading.

Eladia smiled at last and ran her hand through the boy's dark curls as she stood up. She took her letters from Carmen, placed them in the pocket of her apron, and told Paul to get the milk from the icebox.

"We will not have any sugar until the new ration stamps arrive, but we have milk and coffee," she said. "Hurry up!"

Paul ran to the wooden cabinet where a large block of ice kept the milk fresh, while Eladia went about making coffee. Paul peppered her with questions about his mother and their long-ago life in Spain. Smiling at the memories, Eladia told her grandson about Pilar and his Aunt Trini living in Vitoria-Gasteiz over the tavern, and how they liked to hide behind the bar while their father poured drinks.

"I can't imagine them ever playing like that," Paul said as they sat down with their matching cups of café con leche. "They are so serious all the time."

Eladia laughed. "Children never think their parents were once fun people," she said. "Why even I was once a young lady who danced and played piano. I even met the Queen of Spain when I was just a little older than you are now!"

Paul was shocked by this revelation. "You met a real queen?" he asked.

"Yes, yes, I did," Eladia said, her voice softening, and she stared out the window. Silence fell for a few minutes. Then Eladia shook herself from the daydream and examined her empty cup.

"But that was a lifetime ago, and a world I did not like very much. My parents had the wrong expectations for me," she said to her grandson. "At least now, we make our own decisions. And I have decided it's time for you to take a bath." She smiled as Paul grumbled and handed over his cup.

VICTORIA
November 1944
Fallon, Nevada

"Annie, you go ask the gypsy about Fabian."

Victoria nudged her daughter in the side, encouraging her to walk to the fortune teller's booth at the carnival at the Fallon fairgrounds.

"Mom, you are so superstitious! You are afraid of the gypsies when they pass our house on the highway, but now you want me to pay money to talk to one? That doesn't make any sense!" Annie sounded unusually upset, but Victoria did not want to hear any disagreement. Fabian had been shipped to somewhere in the South Pacific and every day the news on the radio was about how terrible the fighting would be there.

Victoria nudged her daughter forward into the little tent and stood just outside the doorway where she could still see inside. If only she could understand the conversation—but it was all in English.

Annie was right: Victoria was afraid of the gypsy people who had roamed the country during the Depression and even now during the war. She was convinced they would steal from her house. Once, when Annie had been left alone at home during the morning milking, a caravan had stopped in the yard. Victoria had dropped the cream separator in her race to get home before Annie could be kidnapped, an event she was certain would have transpired had she not made the dash, ruining a day's milking. But that was then, and now she needed comforting. She was worried about her son, and if the gypsy could see the future, Victoria was willing to pay for the knowledge.

Annie stood up and walked outside, a look of fear on her face.

"What did she say?" Victoria asked, her voice loud and shaking to match the fear on Annie's face.

"She didn't tell me anything!" Annie said angrily. "She kept asking me questions, when I thought I was supposed to be asking her for information. She scared me!"

"What did she say about Fabian?"

Annie looked down at her feet.

"I didn't ask," she whispered. "I just left."

Anger replaced the fear Victoria was feeling. She had spent some hard-earned money to learn whatever she could about the future, and Annie had wasted it.

"This war is going to kill me – and thanks to you, now I will die with no money!" She slapped Annie gently on the back of her head and walked away. Her daughter trailed along behind.

As the war approached the third anniversary of the attack on Pearl Harbor, it had overtaken all aspects of Victoria's life. Fabian was somewhere in a part of the world she had never heard of before, where it seemed there was endless ocean and only a few islands. Both her sons-in-law had been drafted, though thankfully they were still stationed on bases in America. Their wives, Victoria's daughters Polly and Jessie, had moved in together in Winnemucca to save on expenses. Only Tony and Annie were safe in Fallon, where she could keep a watchful eye on them.

Victoria lived for the arrival of V-mail, tiny photographs of the letters Fabian would write, miniaturized by the military to reduce the size and weight of so much mail going back and forth between the troops and their loved ones. She saved each piece of V-mail in one of the storage trunks that had come with the Bassett house, and she used them to remind Annie about the seriousness of the situation.

Just last week, Annie had received a letter from a boy she had known in school, whom she and her friends called "Junior" because his Japanese surname sounded something like the month of June. The boy had graduated earlier in the year, joined the Army, and been deployed to Florida. Victoria knew the boy and his family were Japanese, so she would not let Annie write back to him.

"Those people are trying to kill your brother," she had said, pointing to Fabian's V-Mail letters for emphasis.

"Mom, that's not fair," Annie had whined. "Junior was born in America. He's as American as I am—and he joined the Army to fight the Germans and the Japanese!"

Annie had gone on to explain that the students at her high school had voted Junior the best-liked student in his class. Even the school principal, Walter Johnson, had declared, "My friends, this is democracy in action" at that year's graduation. But Victoria had not wanted to hear about democracy, or the difference between this young man and the people her son was hurtling toward in the escalating conflict. She wanted normalcy and reassurances, even if she had to traffic with gypsies to get the latter.

"Go find your father," she told Annie once the girl had caught up to her at the carnival. "He was resting over by that Ferris wheel contraption. I will be waiting in the car. We are going to stop at church and light a candle on the way home. Something bad is going to happen."

"Mom, how do you know that?" Annie asked in an exasperated tone.

"The chickens are laying eggs with spots of blood in them," Victoria explained. "It means someone is going to die. I am worried about Fabian! Now, find your father. Be quick."

ANNIE

January 1945

Fallon, Nevada

"Get in the car! Pop died this morning. I've been looking all over for you!"

I think most people take a lot of care with how they break bad news to kids, but my sister-in-law Van was pretty upset by the time she broke the news of my father's death to me.

My dad died on January 4, 1945. On January 2, the day after his 59th birthday, he had surgery in the local Handley Hospital. The surgery was for intestinal adhesions caused from previous surgeries for all his stomach troubles. Two days later he developed an embolism and died.

I had gone to school as normal that morning. My mother was at the hospital with Tony and Van, and my sister Polly had come down from Winnemucca. When Pop died, Van was sent to find me and tell me what happened. It was lunch hour and I had walked downtown with some of my friends. Van apparently went first to the high school and couldn't find me. She was quite flustered to begin with, as she had backed her car into someone else's car that morning, and Pop's death had shocked them all. Then when she couldn't find me at school, she was dashing down Maine Street and spotted me walking along with my friends. She pulled over to the curb, opened the car door, and changed my life forever.

I don't remember anyone paying any special attention to me over the following days, except my cousin Modesto, who kept slapping me across the shoulders and saying, "Stand up straight." He wasn't much comfort.

Less than two weeks after my father died, Mom sold our ranch for $6,000. Mom got a down payment of $3,000, and the rest was to be paid in January every year. We moved in with Tony and Van until Mom could find a house in town, close to shopping.

Neither of us could drive, so Mom sold our 1929 Chevy to a friend of Tony's for a hundred dollars. All the farm equipment stayed with the ranch and most of the furniture as well. I took the little blue trunk I had painted to match my bedroom. My mother took two big trunks, one filled with a set of encyclopedias which I had found in the cellar. We also moved an old-fashioned desk with a matching mirror, and our radio, mostly because it reminded me of Pop. My dad listened to the radio all the time and he followed everything that was reported about the war. He knew just what was going on and where the fighting was and understood all the strategies being carried out for the war effort.

It was all over in less than a month.

VICTORIA
August 1945
Fallon, Nevada

Victoria had spent the seven months since her husband's death coming to terms with her old life and starting a new one. A summertime trip to Winnemucca to visit her daughter, Polly, had resulted in the removal of all her teeth—casualties of a life lived without dental care. She quite liked her new dentures. She had also gone dress shopping with Polly.

"Mom, you can put away the denim farm pants for good," Polly had said. "No matter where you and Speed end up living, you're not going to be doing any farm work ever again."

After some consideration, Victoria had agreed. The war in Europe had ended. She was hopeful about the future, even while she grieved Victor's death. And she for once was feeling more comfortable about money.

Victor's brother-in-law, Juan, had come to visit her at Polly and George's house. He had heard of Victor's death and wanted Victoria to have a hundred dollars, saying it was her dead husband's share of the family house in Ea that his sisters had sold. Victoria took the money and thanked her brother-in-law.

Some of the money had gone toward purchasing several new dresses, all of them in dark colors, and three white dickeys—collars that folded out of the top of the dresses' necklines. Victoria liked the look of a clean white dickey next to her face.

"We should get your hair permed, too," Polly announced on the day before Victoria returned by train to Fallon.

Victoria, who had never been to a beauty parlor, protested at first, but then shrugged her shoulders and went along with the plan. She rather enjoyed her new life, and while her superstitions were always close at hand, she found herself relaxing into her changed circumstances.

Two weeks later, Victoria sat in the living room at Tony and Van's, smoothing the skirt of her dark dress with the white dickey, and fiddling with the hairnet that held her permanent in place. She felt like a different person, but the news before her in the telegram was all too familiar—and just as shattering as when she discovered Manuel had contracted the Spanish flu.

"Your son Fabian Rubianes considered seriously ill at this hospital. Recovery questionable," the telegram in her lap read—or so Van had told her.

"But the last telegram said he was not hurt that bad," she argued with her daughter-in-law. "Fabian sent two letters saying not to worry. Why is it bad now?" She did not add that there had been no other sign, no evil talisman or warning to alert her to the now impending doom. As much as she had worried about her son, the news that his condition was so critical took her by surprise.

But now it was clear. No amount of new clothing or hair care could change the facts for Victoria: Fabian had been shot during heavy fighting on Okinawa on May 11. It had taken a month for the news to reach her, and then the telegram had described him as "slightly wounded." Fabian himself had indeed sent word that he felt fine and admonished, "Don't come see me yet." He had been returned stateside and was being cared for at the military hospital in Modesto, California. Then, suddenly, this telegram from the hospital had arrived. Fabian was fighting for his life.

"It is a good thing I look like a city woman now," Victoria said to Van. "I am going to see my son in this city where all the soldiers are being cared for. Tell Tony he will have to drive me."

***

The hospital proved to be a horror show of wounded men. Fabian was barely awake when Victoria and Tony visited, and he said nothing. Victoria wasn't sure he recognized her. Morphine was administered four times a day, penicillin daily. His delirium was nearly constant, and he weighed less than 80 pounds, including the weight of a full-body cast. He had lost all his hair; his skin was practically the color of coal.

From the nursing staff, Victoria learned Fabian's tank had been attacked and, as he and the troops tried to escape, they were cut down by machine gun fire. When he was carried to the field station on Okinawa, where the fighting was still ongoing, he had eleven bullets in his right leg, two in his right elbow, and his stomach and back were full of shrapnel. He had been transferred to a hospital elsewhere in the South Pacific before being flown to San Francisco with other wounded soldiers.

Much of Fabian's body was in a cast when Victoria had arrived at his bedside, but an attending physician told her they might be forced to amputate the leg if his condition did not improve.

"Mrs. Rubianes, I have to tell you, it will be a miracle if he lives," the doctor said in a quiet but firm voice.

Tony translated for his mother while the doctor waited patiently. Before Tony could finish, a nurse ran into the room. She was out of breath.

"The President just announced they dropped some sort of atomic bomb, something huge, right on the Japs!" she blurted.

As the doctor tried to get more information, Victoria tugged on Tony's shirt sleeve and pointed at the nurse. Tony translated the news about the bombing as best he could. Victoria took another look at Fabian, an emaciated form she could hardly recognize.

"Good," was all she said.

ELADIA

October 1945
Reno, Nevada

"Your father nearly killed us on the drive," Eladia declared as she stepped into the small apartment Trini and Carmen shared. "Twenty-five years in this country, and that man still drives like a farmer on a backroad in Spain!"

Trini and Carmen laughed, welcoming their flustered mother to their home. Marcelino had dropped Eladia at the corner before proceeding to an appointment with a doctor for his recurring back pain and a growth on his foot.

"Oh, Mama, you know it's not that bad," said Trini with a laugh. "Have a cup of coffee and put your feet up."

"Tell us about the news from home," Carmen added enthusiastically.

Carmen had moved to Reno the prior year, following her graduation from Churchill County High School. A hard worker and excellent student, she had obtained a credential as a legal secretary in the high school's vocational education program and quickly found a job working for a Reno judge. Trini, who was still working as a salesclerk in various retail stores, made room in her tiny apartment for her baby sister. They rarely traveled home to Fallon and hence needed to hear the news from the ranch.

"Nothing," Eladia said, scowling. "Nothing is new. It is just me and Papa now, and the ranch is not doing well because his health is not good. Jose Luis spends all his time with Tony and Pilar. Thank the Virgin I have Paul, and occasionally his brothers, to keep me company."

Eladia noticed that her daughters rolled their eyes. She wished she were as glib as her husband, a masterful storyteller. She tried another tact.

"I had a letter from Spain, at long last," she said. "It took months to get here, and it had taken my brother months before that even to think to write to me." She paused for effect.

"*Tía* Feliciana is dead."

Trini gasped. She had vague memories of her mother's sisters and brothers, and always enjoyed her mother's reports about life in Spain. The Spanish Civil War had brought terrible tales, but all in all, the Aguirres had done well.

Carmen rolled her eyes a second time. Never having met the Spanish relatives, they were nothing but names to her.

"Which one is she?" Carmen asked, reaching for the coffee pot.

Eladia set her jaw and refused to answer.

"She is the nun, Carmen. She entered the convent during the Civil War." Trini was patient and waited for Eladia to recover so she could finish the story.

"Yes," Eladia said at last. "And because of Franco, she is dead. Malnutrition. In a convent! Who starves a nun?" Eladia looked at her daughters as if expecting an answer. Neither woman spoke.

"Well, it is very sad," said Eladia. "But you wanted the news, and there it is. Now, pour me some coffee and tell me about your jobs."

Conversation quickly turned to lighter matters. Eladia listened in rapt attention as Trini described the world of the J.C. Penney department store and Carmen spoke of her job at the district court. When Carmen announced she was thinking of moving to Washington, D.C., things turned quiet again for almost a full minute. The girls fidgeted as they waited for Eladia's reaction.

"You will do no such thing."

Eladia was firm. Her youngest child was talented, she knew, and aspired to interesting work in business or politics. She was perhaps the most ambitious of all the Erquiaga children. But Washington was too far away.

"How about San Francisco?" offered Carmen, her lips curling in a smile. "That's not so bad, Mama, is it?"

Eladia drank her coffee and tried not to think of her own parents condemning the dreams of her youth. As much as she didn't want to sound like her mother, she found the words coming from her mouth to be reminiscent of too many conversations in her youth.

"There is work here in Reno, and even in Fallon. Amelio Bell came by the house yesterday, asking about you. He is a nice boy. Maybe you can go on a date when you come for Christmas."

Trini and Carmen exchanged glances.

Eladia understood the look between her two daughters, and she hastened to register her disagreement.

"You are coming home for Christmas." It was not a question. Eladia set down her coffee cup with a loud thud.

"My two sons will not be home for months, even though the war with those horrible Germans and the Japanese has ended. But I will have my daughters who live in Reno home for Christmas," Eladia declared. She stared at her daughters, both of whom were inspecting the floor.

"Have I mentioned how sick your father has been? Maybe that will get you home, if not because of me." She paused.

"Yes, Mama," the sisters said in unison.

Eladia took another sip of her coffee.

"Then it is settled." She smiled, but it was her mother's smile, and she knew it.

ANNIE
May 1946
Fallon, Nevada

I ran for a student body office in my junior year of high school. The position of yearbook editor was not often hotly contested, but I had beaten a senior and was quite pleased with myself. My friend Jeneece was elected business manager for the yearbook at the same time. Between us, we practically set out to reinvent the wheel. We were sure nothing was beyond us, and that year of work had proven us correct.

In our freshman and sophomore years, the school did not put out a regular yearbook. Because of the war there was a paper shortage, and so they printed a small booklet on newsprint rather than on glossy paper. Jeneece and I had decided to try to get our year's edition done as it had been prior to 1943: regular size and on glossy paper. Miss Anne Gibbs, the faculty adviser, encouraged us to go ahead. We had no problems getting it done because Mr. Allan Dalbey of one of the town's newspapers, *The Fallon Eagle,* somehow took care of everything. It came out looking great, and that lead to our next big project: We decided to print a school newspaper that year. It was called the *Greenwave Flash.* I loved the writing, and even the production was sort of fun. We typed stencils for each edition and ran it off on the school mimeograph machine.

Those two successes led to me getting a job at the other newspaper in town, *The Fallon Standard.* The office was close to the house Mom had bought on Broadway Street after my dad died. She had chosen the location so she could walk to the Kent's grocery store, but it also meant I could walk to work.

I liked living in town because sometimes my friends could come by after school and we'd do homework together. Jeneece was a coffee drinker, too, and we would make a pot of coffee and drink it while we did our homework. Jeneece worked at the telegraph company for Mrs. Adele Born. Because of our jobs, we couldn't get together as often as we might have otherwise, but when we did, you can bet we compared notes about our highfalutin city jobs!

The Fallon Standard was owned by Claude and Ethel Smith, a husband-and-wife team. My job was connected with the vocational education class at school. Everyone studied something different, a career of their choice, and after my success with journalism and publishing the yearbook, and those short stories I wrote as a young girl, I wanted to be a writer.

My vocational education teacher, Mr. Crawford, was a serious man; I don't remember seeing him smile once all year. But he helped me get my job, and it was a great setup. As soon as class time was over, we all took off for our respective jobs. At first, I worked in the office at the newspaper, not covering the news. Sometimes I typed letters for Mr. Smith. He could type, too, but he only used his two index fingers. I didn't know anyone else who could type as fast the conventional way as he did with just two fingers, but since he was paying me to type, he usually turned the letters over to me.

On Tuesday nights we printed the newspaper, which came out on Wednesday mornings. David Swenson and Connie Madsen worked in the back room on the printing end of the operation. A man whose name I have forgotten set the type on lead slugs, and then Mr. Smith, with help from Connie and Dave, set the lead slugs into columns. They printed a sheet, the office staff would proofread it, and the presses would roll out all the copies. Helen and Beverly Rice lived next door to the newspaper office and they would come in and help Connie, Dave, and me. We would put each paper together, fold it, put an address label on it, and have it ready to go in the morning.

Most of the time I worked for Mrs. Smith. She and Marguerite Lima were on the phone all afternoon calling everyone they could think of to find out what they had been doing. Most people didn't mind having news about themselves printed in the paper, but this wasn't always the case.

One time they sent me out to get a story, but the fellow I tried to interview didn't want his news printed. News had spread around town that a couple of high school students had gotten married. Since I knew the guy from school, the ladies at work decided I should get the story from him, even though I was just an office girl. Well, I was happy to go off with my notebook and pencil in hand to get my first big scoop. But I got fooled, because he looked me straight in the eye and said, "Well, Speed, I don't have any idea what you are talking about. I didn't get married."

I was crushed not to get the story, especially when we found out the next month that he and the girl from school did get married. They just didn't want the whole world to know about it.

Besides the occasional story for Mrs. Smith and Mrs. Lima, I was in charge of maintaining the servicemen's file. Even though the war was over, men were still in the service, and there were lots of stories about what they were doing. All that small-town stuff was of interest because everyone in Fallon knew everyone else. Mrs. Smith had been keeping a file on locals in the service, and the editors often referred to it for stories, so keeping that up to date became my job. "I think we need to include an update on your brother," Mrs. Smith said to me one day. "Aren't the military hospitals closing? What is his health like?"

I cringed on the inside and tried not to show any change of facial expression. Bob had indeed been moved from the Army hospital in Modesto to one in Salt Lake City, and when that closed he was sent to Letterman General Hospital at the Presidio in San Francisco.

"He's getting better, ma'am," was all I could think to say. "But I don't think my mother would like to have that written about." I paused, pleading with my eyes, and thinking about that young couple and their own news that they hadn't wanted to see in the paper.

"News is news, Anita," Mrs. Smith said. "Write it up."

***

I worked at the paper right up to my high school graduation. There was plenty to do and I needed the money, as I had begun to make plans for after high school.

I got 50 cents an hour and a copy of the newspaper for my work. I had saved as much of this money as I could because my teacher, Anne Gibbs, was encouraging me to go to college. She helped me apply for a Fleischman Scholarship, worth $400, and it was awarded before graduation. I really wanted to go to the university in Reno and study journalism. To be on the safe side, I also took the State Merit Exam, which qualified me for employment with the State of Nevada.

Mom and I had long talks about whether I could afford to go to college or should take a job with the State in Carson City. Mom thought a job that paid a salary was a better bet, and we still didn't know what would happen with Bob, if and when he got to come home, so two days after my birthday I accepted a position with the Employment Security Department in Carson City. Anne Gibbs was crushed that I didn't go to college, but she helped me, and three or four other Fallon girls, find housing in Carson for our new lives.

I loved my new setup! I lived in a boarding house run by a couple, Jim and Alice Gladding. Mrs. Gladding provided breakfast and dinner, and we had to eat lunch downtown. The boarding house was only two blocks from the state capitol, where I worked in the building called the annex. My bedroom was in the attic, and it had a sloping ceiling. There was one large bathroom downstairs that we all shared, and a room next to that with a wringer washing machine and big tubs where we did our laundry.

One of the first people I met in Carson City was Ivy May Maddaford. We both worked at Employment Security, in the section where people's unemployment checks were processed; a couple of my friends worked in the section where they determined whether people were eligible for support. Not long after we were hired—at what was for me an astronomical salary of $185 a month—the man who ran Employment Security, Gilbert C. Ross, died most unexpectedly and we got a new boss. Denver Dickerson had served as Speaker of the Nevada Assembly and his dad had been governor about the time my parents came to this country. Mr. Dickerson was a serious man, but he was kind to all us girls. Because I had so much experience as a writer, he occasionally gave me special writing projects like reports to the legislature. I quizzed him about politics whenever I had the chance.

In November, George Frey was elected to represent Fallon in the state assembly. Although George was a bit older than me, I had met him during my days with the *Fallon Standard*, so when he showed up in Carson, I didn't waste any time reintroducing myself. He was a Republican. My boss and my boss's boss, Governor Vail

Pittman, were Democrats, and that led George and me to have some lively discussions about what the administration was doing and what the legislature wanted. I decided I was a Republican, too. I also introduced George to my friend, Elenor, who was working at Employment Security with me. They really hit it off. Just as important, George became a dependable ride home when I needed to hitch a ride back to Fallon to see Mom.

One of the girls who lived at the Gladdings' boarding house with me left to attend university, but the rest of us girls stayed at our jobs. Although I was envious of her college plans, I really liked living in Carson and having my horizons broadened by interacting with people who were so different. It was a small town and friendly because everyone knew everyone else. For the first time in my life, I felt like I was part of the "in" crowd. I really developed a taste for politics.

VICTORIA
April 1947
Fallon, Nevada

Victoria and Bob sat on the porch at Tony and Van's house. Bob had arrived home from Letterman Hospital the week before and, although there was not much room in Victoria's tiny house, he was—as he put it—"bunking" with her. It was nice to get outside, and there was a lush green lawn around the house. Bob's crutches were leaned against the wall of the house behind them.

"When is Speed coming home from Carson?" Bob asked his mother.

"She will not be home until next weekend," Victoria replied. "This week she is going to Lake Tahoe with her friends. Swimming, I think."

"Must be nice." Bob sounded uninterested.

Victoria nodded. "You remember Anna Legarza? She grew up in Winnemucca. She is a cousin to your cousin Modesto, but no relation to us."

Bob made no sound. He stared off into the distance.

"Well, she also lives in Carson City, and she has been looking after Annie. She and Annie are part of something to do with the Catholic Church, and some girls are showing Annie around. They went to Reno and gambled at the Mapes Casino once!"

Victoria smiled and tried to make eye contact with her son.

"Your sister is living the high life," she continued. "She met the governor the other day, and she is always going to some dance, or picnic, or activity with her friends. You should be happy for her."

Bob finally looked over at his mother.

"Should I?" His tone was bitter.

The smile disappeared from Victoria's face.

"Well, I am happy for her," she said. "She will come home to see you next weekend when she can—" Victoria switched to English.

"Hitch a ride?" At Bob's nod, she returned to speaking Basque. "Yes, she will come see you then."

Van emerged from the house as Victoria finished her sentence. She was carrying a pitcher of lemonade and a wooden tray with glasses on it.

"You must be talking about Speed," Van said with a smile. "She sure is growing up. Bob, you know Pilar Ormachea. My friend from the telephone company? The one whose husband died, and she moved back here?"

Bob did not respond.

"Pilar is an Erquiaga and her sisters, Carmen and Trini, are taking Speed to San Jose this summer for a conference for Young Leadership Institute—YLI, they call it. It's all Speed talks about."

"I already told him about that group," Victoria said, her exasperation finally showing. "He is in a bad mood and doesn't care."

Van winced. "Well, Mom, we will just have to lighten the mood. Maybe we can plan a trip to see Uncle Pete!"

Victoria's brother, Pete, lived in Winnemucca, his sheepherding days behind him. He was often with his niece, Polly, and her husband. It had been nearly a year since Victoria had seen her brother.

"How the hell are you gonna get me to Winnemucca?" Bob asked Van in English. He gestured toward his crutches and then at the stub of a remaining leg.

"You take train," Victoria answered, also in English, her expression making it clear that she understood more than her son thought. "I can. You can."

"Well, hell," Bob said with a laugh, still in English. "I guess you told me! Got any beer to go with that lemonade, Van?"

Victoria did not understand everything he said, but she liked the change in mood.

"Beer!" she said, and pointed at her chest, then at Bob's.

All three laughed. Talk turned to the train ride and, as Bob's demeanor thawed, Van broached the subject of him learning to drive, even with a disability.

"Yeah, they've got a lot of programs for veterans," Bob agreed. "I will look into it, I guess."

"More beer," Victoria said with a renewed laugh.

ANNIE
December 1947
Fallon, Nevada

"I feel like celebrating!" I told my friend Ivy. "We both got raises today. We're going to be making a whopping $235 a month! Let's stop and get dinner while we are so rich."

Ivy Maddaford and I walked home from the capitol every day, most days gossiping about politicians or our dreams for the future as we walked. Ivy and I were always together, and I feel that she changed my outlook on life more than anyone else ever had. She had grown up in such a different world than I had, and she introduced me to another lifestyle altogether. Her parents were from England, and her father had worked in mining in Ruth, Nevada. When he retired, they moved to Carson, so Ivy still lived at home. They were nice people who had taken me under their wing almost like one of their kids.

Ivy's family was not Catholic, so she was not a part of Young Leadership Institute with me, Anna Legarza, and the Fallon gang. Instead, Ivy and I joined a sorority called Beta Sigma Phi. It was in no way connected with college or college sororities. There were two or three chapters in Carson. That was an interesting experience for me. I met a lot of people that I would not have known otherwise. They had a lot of formal affairs and they had some study groups. It was great to have the opportunity to dress up in our formal dresses occasionally. The sorority was instrumental in bringing some singing groups into Carson, and of course Ivy and I were always there to see the performances.

I was still living at the boarding house, and I loved it. Jim and Alice Gladding rented five rooms to single women working in Carson. The house was about two blocks west of the Dutch Mill. Jeneece and some other girls from high school were all working in Carson, living around town with other families. I learned a lot from the people who took us country girls into their homes, and from Ivy's family. Table manners and social etiquette were new to me, but thanks to those friends and families, I was able to hold my own at political dinners around town. When the legislature was in session, we rubbed elbows with a lot of interesting people—and I was able to use the right fork for the right food!

"Now that we are women of the world, we can buy more silverware," Ivy proclaimed when we sat down to dinner the day we got our raises.

Ivy had convinced me to buy silverware for my future home. I had never heard of such a thing, but she explained you could pay for pieces over time. I had only been able to scrape together enough money for two place settings by that point, but Ivy figured that our raises meant we could now afford one place setting each month.

I had chosen a pattern called Grand Baroque made by Wallace. It was very ornate, and I just loved it, even though Ivy pointed out it was a pattern that would require an elaborate home and lifestyle to go with it. But did I understand that? Of course not. I just knew I loved it, and I was sometimes willing to forsake new clothes to come up with the thirty-five dollars a month that it took to buy a place setting.Ivy and I had each bought a Lane cedar chest, too, and we put our silver in there as we brought each setting home. There was also a sort of selling club going around the office that you could pay into each week, and after a certain number of weeks you owned a blanket, or a set of sheets, or a down comforter. We tried them all and soon our cedar chests got pretty full. Ivy's family and the folks at the boarding house teased us because neither of us even had a boyfriend, but we had our dowries!

When our celebratory dinner was done, Ivy wanted to know what I was doing for Christmas.

"Going home to Fallon," I said. "I already found a ride. I'm not looking forward to it, though."

***

As I was afraid, Christmas was different that year. My sister, Jessie, had a one-year-old daughter, Judy, and they came to Fallon from their home in Winnemucca. I'd always been the baby in the family and, even though I was now 19 years old, it felt a little strange to be displaced in that role. I hadn't been around Judy much in her first year of life, so I never learned how to change a diaper or hold her head the way you're supposed to with a baby. Judy sure was cute, though, and my feelings of jealousy passed quickly.

There were lots of new people around as well. The Baumans, for example, who were Tony and Van's friends, and to whose place they took us all for Christmas dinner. The Baumans had a large family present, plus all of us. I had never had a holiday with so many people. I didn't know the Bauman kids in school, because they were a few years behind me, but we mixed like old friends that Christmas night. At first, I barely noticed that there was no silverware on the table and no conversation about politics.

Tony made a surprise appearance as Santa Claus, sneaking out after dinner to change into his costume in the car. I remembered the Christmas I'd overheard Jessie and Mom talking about my stocking, and I didn't want to ruin things for the younger folk, so I played along with Tony as best I could. Much to his dismay, Judy was too young to understand, and the three Bauman kids were too old to care. We went home early, with me thinking about the differences between farm life and the city, and between being 19 instead of a kid.

The next morning, I had to get Bob to drive me back to Carson. Bob was still living with Mom and his recovery was going well. He had his own car now, specially outfitted so he could drive with only one leg. We laughed about my poor choice in chauffeurs all the way to the capitol annex, where he dropped me off in time for work. It was hard to admit that Carson felt more like home than Fallon did that Christmas. The next week, I added to my list of activities by joining the Business and Professional Women's Club. I was determined to make a go of this new life in what was for me the big city.

ELADIA
October 1948
Reno, Nevada

Eladia sat in the waiting room at the hospital with her daughter, Trini. Marcelino was having surgery on his foot. Over the last three years, a black lump had grown on the top of his foot and after several visits to doctors in Reno and Woodland, California, the diagnosis had been tuberculosis of the bone.

"Did you ever live in the tropics?" the doctor at the Woodland Clinic had asked.

Marcelino said that he had not, and when the doctor explained that this type of tuberculosis was related to damp living conditions, Marcelino recalled how much time he had spent standing ankle-deep in water when he worked in the mines during his first stint in America, before he returned to Spain to start a family. Whether that was the cause or not, the surgery had been scheduled—and it was expected to have serious ramifications.

"The doctor said he will have to walk with crutches when this over."

Eladia looked over at her daughter, who had tears in her eyes. "Yes, he is not going to be able to work the ranch," Eladia replied. "We are selling it to Uncle Ramon and Tomasa. Well, not so much selling it as having them take it over for the loan they provided during the Depression. They will give us back some of the money we have paid."

"That's very nice of Uncle Ramon," Trini said quietly, taking her mother's hand.

Given the low productivity of the Soda Lake property, Marcelino had not always been able to make the monthly payments to his brother-in-law. He was relieved to be free of the burden, with enough cash in return to rent a little house in town, or maybe find a small place in the country. Eladia was less relieved, feeling the jaws of American life closing around her once more.

"Yes, Ramon is a generous man, thank the Blessed Virgin."

Eladia's irritation about the ranch and her husband's health was mitigated by the fact that her sons were finally home. Joe, Tony, and Louie—Jose Luis having shortened his name—were farming together around the valley. They were jointly running several properties and seemed to be making a good living. Tony had taken advantage of some of the federal government's training programs for veterans to improve his ranching skills. They had even created a cattle brand combining an "E" for Erquiaga with the number three to represent the three brothers.

None of the brothers was married yet, but Eladia had her grandsons close by with Pilar having returned to Fallon upon the sudden death of her husband, and her daughter Mary had one daughter and a son living in Tonopah. Carmen had finally returned to Fallon for work as well, all thoughts of traveling around America gone from her head, and had even gone on a few dates with Amelio Bell. Trini insisted on staying in Reno.

"I will say a prayer for him at Mass this Sunday," said Trini.

"You should join a convent, daughter," her mother said with a smile. She squeezed Trini's hand and sat quietly staring at the door of the waiting room, waiting for the doctor to emerge with news of the surgery. "We could all use your prayers."

**

Several weeks after his surgery, Marcelino was still walking with crutches, so he and Eladia proceeded with the land sale of the Soda Lake property. They also sold their small herd of cattle to their sons and took up residence with Louie at the Ernst Ranch, which the three boys were leasing. For Eladia, it felt like more than an ending to her dreams of land ownership.

"We are entirely dependent on our children," she told Marcelino one day when he was practicing walking around the kitchen with his crutches.

Marcelino bridled at her accusation.

"We have money!" he said. "I have been hiding silver dollars in coffee cans, and there is still some money from the sale of the ranch and the cows."

"How long do you think that will last?" Eladia asked, shaking her head.

Marcelino had no answer.

"We are trapped," Eladia said finally, filling the silence. "My poor mother has died, and I know there is an inheritance for me, but Franco will not allow Spanish banks to transfer any money out of the country. My brother says the money is just sitting there!"

Marcelino shook his head and steered his way through the archway leading from the kitchen to the living room, his crutches clomping loudly on the linoleum floor. "I do not know what you want me to say," he declared.

Eladia had no answer.

ANNIE
Christmas Eve 1948
Fallon, Nevada

We arrived at the Fraternal Hall on Maine Street in Fallon just after nine o'clock in the evening. My sister-in-law Van and I laughed and teased each other as we removed heavy winter coats, dusted with snow from the storm that was slowly covering my tiny hometown with a blanket of white. Hats and scarves found temporary homes on the shelf over the coat hooks, and, with a final check of one another's hair, we plunged into a noisy room of revelers, as my brother, Tony, made a face and laughed a little at our behavior.

"Oh, don't pay attention to him," said Van. "He doesn't have a romantic bone in his body. Let's find Pilar!"

Van linked her arm in mine, and we began our search for Van's friend from work. Tony headed for a group of his friends in one corner of the Hall. Before we could spot her, we heard Pilar Ormachea's voice yelling over the din. "Hey! Over here!"

We joined Pilar by the punch bowl, and she jumped right into a breathless conversation about the weather and the thirty-mile drive from what she jokingly called "the Big City." I knew Pilar because her sisters, Carmen and Trini, were in my YLI group. "I hitched a ride home yesterday with George Frey," I said. "He was in Carson for a meeting, thank goodness. Now that he won't be going back to the legislature for the next session, I will sure miss having him as my chauffeur!" Pilar and Van knew I couldn't drive anything except a tractor, and I hadn't done that since Pop died. It was common for me to find rides home with folks who worked in Carson when I couldn't enlist my brother Bob as chauffeur.

The three of us shared a laugh or two as glasses of red punch were handed around. Pilar made small talk with Van, comparing notes about their jobs at the phone company. I added a few anecdotes about life in Carson, including how much I loved rubbing elbows with the political crowd, and I shared the gossip about which of my friends had found beaus.

"Didn't you introduce George Frey to his new wife?" Pilar asked. "No wonder he gave you rides home—he owes you!"

It was true, I often took credit for introducing George and my friend, Elenor. Pilar's comment reminded all three of us of why we were at the dance on Christmas Eve: it was meant to be an arranged date, but I was still waiting. An awkward silence fell.

"My brother is late," Pilar finally offered. "He called me at home this afternoon to say he would be here, but . . . something about the cows and the storm and, well, I wasn't really listening." She laughed a little to lighten the mood.

I know the look on my face must have given away my disappointment. I had come home to see Mom and my family for Christmas, of course, but the added excitement that really got me home was to meet Pilar's younger brother, who was also named Tony, like my brother. It had been three months since I broke up with a member of an old Carson family, and—while I wasn't exactly heartbroken—I did want to get back out into the dating world. I suppose I felt left out, at the ripe old age of 20. A lot of my friends were already married, or at least engaged, and it seemed like every Nevada soldier and sailor home from the war had already found his bride.

"He'll be here, don't worry!" Pilar added with enthusiasm. Van nodded reassuringly and rubbed my arm in a companionable way, reaching out to squeeze my hand.Pilar was right, of course. Tony Erquiaga did come to the dance. He walked in when the band was taking a break, and he was covered with snow, wearing his Navy overcoat from his time in the service. He was with his brother, Louie. I knew Louie from school, but because Tony was older than us, I'd never met him. Just as I caught sight of him, someone put a record on the phonograph so the band could enjoy some refreshments, and Tommy Dorsey's song *Until* began to play. It was a big hit that year.

I suppose it's silly, but the words seemed to fit what I hoped was a dramatic moment: "You were sent from Heaven just for me, and you are so heavenly."

It was right about that time that Pilar spilled her punch (sometimes I think on purpose) and Tony came over to rescue her and introduce himself. We quickly found ourselves on the dance floor and I was thrilled to discover that Tony was an excellent dancer. Just after midnight the whole gang went out for a bite to eat. Tony sat next to me, and I could see Van and Pilar begin to conspire about our next outing. I felt like my life was about to change.

PART SIX:

The Americans

1950–1955

PART SIX:
The Americans
1950–1955

ANNIE
National City, California
January 1950

Tony didn't carry me across the threshold of our new home, the way you always hear about grooms doing, but we did make a big production of settling into the house when we arrived, a week after our wedding. Tony had been living in the San Diego area for most of our courtship in 1949. He had given up farming with his brothers and taken a job with Philco Corporation, helping to mothball the Navy fleet, about three months after we met at the Christmas Eve dance. If I had still been writing stories about LaRue Davies and her imaginary friends, that year would have been called *The Matchmakers and the Young Romantics*. Pilar and Van had done their best to ensure Tony and I kept up our dating life, despite the distance, and he had proposed in November when we met up in Los Angeles.

The wedding was held on January 2, after weeks of planning with family and friends. Despite my mother's superstitions about almost having thirteen people at our rehearsal dinner, things went off without a hitch. After a Nuptial Mass at St. Patrick's, we all went to the VFW Hall for a simple lunch of roast turkey and salads. The centerpiece on the lace tablecloth was a round mirror of Van's with the three-tiered cake placed on it and surrounded by white carnations. After lunch we went back to Tony and Van's house and changed clothes, and soon were on our way. Father Mikula had given us five copies of our marriage certificate, saying that we might need to prove we were married to get a motel someplace. I didn't have the heart to disagree with a priest and, sure enough, no one asked.

Our honeymoon consisted of the drive to National City, just outside San Diego. We spent a week getting there, with stops at Hoover Dam, Flagstaff, Oak Creek Canyon, and Jerome, Arizona. We also went to the Grand Canyon, where the deer came up to the car windows looking for a handout of food.

Tony had rented a furnished house for us in National City—a one bedroom, one bath, with a small yard. The only furniture we owned was my cedar chest, which Tony had brought down on the back seat of his car before Christmas, and it fit nicely at the foot of the bed. We had received so many shower and wedding gifts that the rest of the house seemed full and very homey.

"Don't you think I should get a job?" I had asked Tony on the drive down. "You know I can't cook anything but fried potatoes and eggs with cinnamon toast—oh, and hot milk sponge cake. I'm not going to make a very good housewife."

"Married women don't work, even around here," Tony had said.

***

Within a few months, I had learned a lot more about cooking and had gained 12 pounds. Someone had given me *The Joy of Cooking* at the wedding shower Ivy threw for me, and even though it didn't have any pictures of the dishes, I had no trouble picking out things that were good.

I also learned to drive. The clutch was the hard part, but Tony was a patient teacher. We took turns driving around the countryside, sightseeing. Our green Nash Rambler could be made into a bed by folding down the backseat, so we went camping sometimes. We even went to Tijuana, across the border in Mexico, to see the horse and dog races and a bullfight. Tony thought I would hate seeing the bull being killed, but I guess I had seen worse growing up on a farm, because it didn't bother me. It was all part of the new experiences in my life, and I loved everything about the things we got to do. I may have missed my job and the gals in Carson, but I loved my new life of leisure.

In Tijuana, there were booths along the sidewalks, where people sold everything you could imagine. We didn't try the food, but Tony was taken with these little things made of walnuts. They looked like pigs—with ears and a snout that moved, and four legs made of toothpicks. Tony said they had Mexican jumping beans in them, and we bought two. They stopped jumping a few days after we got home. Tony opened them up and found a dead fly inside. Apparently, that was what made them jump!

We also spent money on more practical things. One of the first things we bought was a sewing machine. It was Tony's idea. We went to a Singer store downtown, but the salesman said he would come to the house for a demonstration. Tony told me that was how his father and mother met in Spain, and I suppose the romance of their story carried us away, because we spent $150 on a Singer Featherweight.

Once we had it delivered, Tony could not stop talking about all the things the new machine could do. One of his friends at work wanted to see, in case his wife wanted one, and Tony demonstrated everything it was capable of—just like the salesman had. He should have gotten part of the commission when our friends bought one, too! Fortunately for me, our purchase came with ten free sewing lessons, because I hadn't touched a sewing machine since my ill-fated attempt at making a pantsuit in high school home economics.

I felt very settled in my new domestic life, and we continued to enjoy the experiences of a big city. The Philco crew that Tony worked with were mostly married men, and I got to know their wives. Sure enough, they also didn't have jobs. Together, we learned to host dinner parties and play a card game called Canasta. I was soon feeling like my young social self and remembering that my parents told me not to be afraid of anything.

That first summer in California, one of the Philco wives had a new baby girl, and I decided I wanted to go to the hospital to visit her. I thought my driving was up to par at this point and, since Tony had been sent up the coast to Long Beach to work for a couple days, I took the car and headed out on my own. I knew the general direction where Mercy Hospital in San Diego was located, but I didn't realize how far away it really was. After a while, I could still see the hospital in the distance, but I was no longer in familiar territory. I couldn't decide how to get there but figured I could retrace my tracks back to our house, so I turned around. Thankfully, I made it without mishap.

When Tony came home and I told him about my adventure, he just looked at me with a strange expression on his face and said, "Well, you couldn't have gotten there at all from where you were. We have never been over in that area." He was very calm. And that was a relief.

ELADIA
Fallon, Nevada
March 1951

The Erquiaga family had called a meeting to discuss Joe's health and what it meant for the future. Every member of the clan who lived in Fallon gathered at the little house on the Kinney Ranch where Marcelino and Eladia had been living for a year as part of the larger living and ranching arrangement managed by their sons, Joe and Louie. Eladia was uneasy about just how this meeting might go, but when the discussion began, she was relegated to the kitchen to make coffee and set a few sugar cookies on a plate.

Joe had been sick since January, and a doctor in Riverside, California, had finally diagnosed Joe as having a heart condition. The doctor added to his diagnosis what felt like a death sentence to the family's dreams: Joe should stop working immediately, and could expect never to work again, lest he suffer a heart attack and die. The death of Pilar's husband in 1947 still loomed large for the entire family. After three years as a telephone operator in Fallon, Pilar had only recently moved back to Susanville with her three boys in search of better opportunities. No one wanted that for Joe's wife, Elizabeth, and their young son, Michael.

Joe and Louie had been running two larger ranches together, the Ernst place and the Belaustegui place. Louie was single, so he lived in the tiny ramshackle house on the Belaustegui Ranch, while Joe and his family lived in the old Ernst house. The Kinney Ranch was adjacent to the Ernst place, and Marcelino—recovered from his tuberculosis of the bone but still suffering from a bad back—was able to pitch in a little money made from trapping gophers, and Eladia's egg business and gardening kept them fed. The dramatic change in Joe's circumstances, however, no doubt would alter the arrangements for them all.

Eladia carried a plate of cookies into the living room and placed it on the coffee table. She gestured to her daughter, Carmen, to join her in the kitchen. Carmen's husband, Amelio "Bill" Bell, remained with Marcelino, Joe, and Louie for the discussion.

"What do you think is going to happen?" Eladia asked her daughter as they gathered a few coffee cups. "And why did they send Elizabeth away?"

Carmen shook her head.

"Mama, Elizabeth offered to take Irene and Mike back to her place because the kids make too much noise. This is important. And before you ask again, I don't know what they will decide. It's a terrible problem to have."

Carmen, Bill, and their one-year-old, Irene, lived with Bill's mother on their family ranch across town. The young couple had known each other most of their lives and Eladia had been relieved when they were married the year before, just a month after Tony and Anita. Carmen was well cared for, Eladia knew. The same might not be said for Elizabeth if anything were to happen to Joe; that much she understood.

The coffee made and the cups stacked on a tray for serving, the two women returned to the living room. Eladia made a point of drawing a chair from the dining table up next to her husband and asked Carmen to pour the coffee.

"Have a cookie," she said to Marcelino, and she folded her hands in her lap.

"Papa . . . uh, Mama . . . Elizabeth and I have made a decision."

Joe's voice was slow and uncertain. He spoke Spanish so his parents could understand.

"We are going to move to town and give up the Ernst place."

Marcelino slapped his right knee with one hand and began speaking rapidly. He supported the decision but wanted to know what it meant for Louie.

"Louie cannot run the Belaustegui place and this place all by himself," Marcelino declared. "It is too much, and I am too frail to be of any real help."

Louie nodded.

"We know, Papa, we know. I called Tony last night and we talked about it. He doesn't really like living in Southern California—says it gives him a stomachache all the time—so he and Anita will move back and run the Belaustegui place. She was born when her family lived there. It's kind of funny . . ."

Louie looked like he was winding up to tell a long-winded joke in the form of a tangential story, so Eladia cut him off.

"What about us?" she asked. "That has to be the point of this meeting."

She looked accusingly at her sons.

Marcelino interjected.

"I have two coffee cans buried in the yard, each of them filled with silver dollars," he said. "We can help out."

Louie laughed. "Papa, you've been hiding those cans since the Depression."

"I thought they might come in handy!" exclaimed Marcelino.

Joe swallowed before interrupting his father and brother's discussion.

"We think you should move in with Louie, Mama." he said after a pause. "He's still a bachelor, and the Ernst house is plenty big for the three of you. We can give up the lease on this place. Louie and Tony can make the other two ranches work if they share equipment and time, the way we've been doing."

"I see," said Eladia before turning to look at Marcelino. "And did you know of this plan?"

Marcelino shook his head.

"No, I did not, but it makes perfect sense. My coffee cans are not very big." He looked defeated even as he voiced agreement.

Carmen leaned forward in her chair.

"It does make sense, Mama. You know Bill and I would love to have you come live with us, but we are still with his mom for a little while longer. We're waiting for the renter to leave the small house they have on the back forty and we'll go there, but it's not as big as the Ernst house. I think this is a good idea." She smiled and nodded encouragingly at her mother.

There was silence for a while, the only sound coming from Louie chewing a cookie.

"Well, if it means Antonio will be home, I guess it's worth it," Eladia finally said. "Carmen, pour me some coffee with milk. Extra sugar."

VICTORIA
Babbitt, Nevada
November 1951

Judy Heinz sat on the floor at her grandmother's feet, silently paging through a picture book. Victoria looked down with a smile. The Thanksgiving turkey was cooking in Jessie's new kitchen, and Victoria was glad not to have had the task of butchering it and cleaning its feathers. She was content with the day.

Bob had driven Victoria, Jessie, and Jessie's daughter, Judy, from Fallon to the house that Eddie Heinz had rented for his family in Babbitt. Eddie had taken a job with the Army Depot, and for the first few weeks there had been no houses available, so his wife and five-year-old daughter lived in Fallon with Victoria. Now that the house was ready, they had gathered under the new roof for Thanksgiving. Polly and George Etchart had driven down from Winnemucca and were staying at the El Capitan hotel across the highway in Hawthorne.

"Grandma, will you read to me?"

Victoria smiled. Unbeknownst to her children, she had been practicing her English using Judy's simple books as a guide. She had begun to dream of becoming a United States citizen after all these years in America, and she knew there would be an exam of some kind. When her husband, Victor, had obtained his citizenship, he had been asked questions by a judge in Winnemucca, and she expected something similar—but she knew there would be something written she would have to study beforehand, so she was slowly teaching herself to read.

"Yes, sit here," she said to Judy in English. She patted her knee.

The child scrambled up and plopped herself on Victoria's lap, resting her head on her grandmother's ample bosom and touching the white lace of the old woman's dickey collar. Victoria smiled at how plump she knew she was becoming, thanks to city living, and took pride in what a comfortable seat she made for the child.

"What this word?" she asked Judy.

As the girl prattled to herself, Victoria turned her attention to the kitchen where her daughters and son were carrying on a lively conversation. George had run to the liquor store with Eddie, so the three Rubianes siblings were on their own. It occurred to Victoria that the conversation didn't need more liquor. It seemed animated enough as it was.

"Some of us don't speak English that fast," she called in Basque to the next room.

"Sorry, Mom," said Bob, switching languages for his mother. "We were just talking about Polly and George's business. Etchart Machinery is making money, and Polly is complaining about taxes!"

"At least you have an income to tax," Victoria admonished. "Some of us are not that lucky." She arched an eyebrow at her eldest daughter and returned her attention to Judy, asking the child—quietly, in English—what a cow said as she pointed at a picture of a milk cow on the pages of the book.

A chastened Polly redirected the conversation, politely speaking in Basque so her mother could follow along.

"Jessie says you have a girlfriend," she said to Bob, a wry smile on her face.

"Jessie has a big mouth," Bob said, glaring at his sisters.

Jessie laughed. "Well, Van told me she introduced you to Gert Jones down at the phone company."

"I already knew Gert," Bob said defensively. "She was in school with us, and you know her brother Ken served in the Army at the same time I did. Besides, we only went on one date."

Polly chuckled as she lit a cigarette and finished her glass of whiskey.

"Well, here comes another six-week marriage," she said.

Bob swore under his breath and Victoria attempted to stop listening. Bob had made a disastrous six-week marriage to a woman in Fallon not long after he returned from the hospital following the war. No one in the family was sure why the spur-of-the-moment marriage had lasted such a short time, and Victoria had no desire to learn more now. There was room for her son in the tiny house she owned, and she was content to have him there.

"It is too bad Annie and Tony couldn't come for Thanksgiving," she said to no one in particular, attempting to change the subject.

Jessie heard the deflection for what it was and joined in.

"She said they are going to spend Thanksgiving with Tony and Van, Mom. They will be fine there. Besides, she is busy working on their house."

Polly snorted and took a drag on her cigarette.

"How can they live in that place? It hasn't changed since we lived there before the Depression," she said, her tone judgmental.

"They are doing the best they can," Jessie said. "We have all lived in some pretty rough places."

Bob shook his head.

"Going to be hard to bring a baby home to a place that doesn't have a bathroom," he said.

ANNIE
Fallon, Nevada
April 1952

I had not wanted to leave California at first when Tony's brothers called him home to run one of the ranches they had on lease. But once we got back to Nevada, I decided it was nice to be so close to family, and I threw myself into the role of farmwife. A big part of it was fixing up our home. It was strange to return to the house where my family had lived when I was born. Fallon was a small place, though, and Basque families stuck together. The Belausteguis, who had rented to my father all those years ago, later rented to the Erquiaga brothers as well. In fact, Tony had been living in the house when we met in 1948.

When my parents moved there in 1928, the house consisted of four rooms: a large kitchen, where we also ate, and three bedrooms. The outside walls of the house were made of one-by-twelve boards with no paint on them. When Tony and I moved in, it was still the same four rooms and weathered boards. I had grown up in the Bassett house, which was no prize, but since 1946 I had lived in one town or another, and I'd grown accustomed to indoor plumbing, heat that didn't come from a wood-burning stove, and a few other "luxuries." So, it was quite a shock when we came to the Belaustegui place in 1951.

Tony had some telephone conversations with Juan Belaustegui about ways to fix up the house. There was even a moment or two when they talked about building a new house, but that fell by the wayside quickly. We were young and in love and starting a new life; it didn't seem like an insurmountable task to just fix up the existing house. And we had help. Charlie Landis was a former miner, part-time farmer, part-time carpenter, and a friend of my brother. He had been hired to add two new rooms to the house and convert one of the original rooms to a bathroom.

With no indoor plumbing, we had an outhouse down by the chicken house. There was a pump house just a few feet away from the kitchen door, and the kitchen did have running cold water. Outside, Tony fixed a makeshift shower, about the size of a regular shower stall. It had a wooden floor and at the top there was a large bowl taken from an old cream separator. There was a spigot which the cream had once come through when it was used as first intended. For our set up, I heated water in the house on the wood-burning stove, lugged it outside in a bucket, and then poured it into the bowl. Then I quickly got into the shower and turned the spigot on so the water would run out. Trying to wash my hair with that small amount of water was a real pain, not to mention the cotton blowing around from all the cottonwood trees on the ranch. Besides that, there were little spiders running all around and I was afraid to look too closely in case there were other bugs. When I got out, I wrapped myself in a towel and put on some slippers, but by the time I got into the house, my feet were covered with dirt and had to be washed again.

Within a few weeks, I had decided that the outdoor shower was ridiculous, and I started going to my mother's house for baths. With our first baby on the way, it became clear that Tony and Charlie had to get the bathroom finished soon.

The house did have electricity, but the wires had been strung across the ceiling in plain sight. Each room had one overhead light in the center of the room, and the kitchen had one over the sink. The kitchen had two outlets and each of the other rooms had one. Tony was familiar with electrical work, so he rewired the whole house with heavier Romex wire—and he put the wires in the attic where they belonged!

The interior walls of all four original rooms of the house were tongue-and-groove boards about three inches wide. Where they each joined, it left about a quarter inch gap the full length of the board. We decided to use spackling compound to fill in these gaps and then we sanded the walls until they were smooth. They didn't look as good as sheetrock (which the two new rooms had) but they did look better than with the gaps. We worked on this together almost every evening. When I had time during the day, I worked at it alone. It was a big job. The smoke from the wood-burning stove had taken a toll on the inside of the house. An area of the kitchen ceiling, about ten square feet around the chimney, was black from the smoke, then it faded out to dark gray and a lighter grey. This all had to be scrubbed away before the ceiling could be painted. The linoleum on the floors was worn completely through to the boards beneath as well. In the kitchen, the linoleum had been glued to the floor, so it was a real chore to get it off. I used an axe and chipped away at it until it came off in little pieces. Wielding my axe, I spent a fair amount of time wondering what Tony had meant when he said "wives don't work" back when we first got married. I felt like I was working plenty!

Since no one had been living in the Belaustegui house for a while when we moved in, various kinds of creatures had made themselves at home around there. One day Tony spotted a snake in the yard that he said was a blue racer. He killed it on the spot because he said it would eat our chicks.

About three weeks later, Tony had gone to the Ernst Ranch to work with Louie, and I was home alone. I walked into the pump house to get something and saw there was another blue racer. I found a shovel near the door and smashed its head, and then I jabbed it in a half dozen more places just in case it wasn't quite dead. I was rather pleased with myself over that. After all, I had never been that close to a snake before. Tony thought it was totally unnecessary that I had jabbed it so many times, but I wasn't going to take any chances. One day I was going to go to town. Tony was working at Louie's place. I got ready to go and headed for the door, and there, along the north wall of the kitchen, was a gopher snake stretched out full length. Tony did not bother to kill gopher snakes. In fact, he usually picked them up with a shovel and a bucket and carried them out to the field someplace to turn them loose. I was less discerning about types of snakes. I was home alone, and I knew I couldn't go off to town and leave the snake in my kitchen, because who knew where he would be by the time I got back. I went outside and found a shovel by the pump house, came back in, and started swinging at the snake. I missed him. He took off for the dining room with me right behind. I watched in dismay as he slithered behind the bookcase, which was against the south wall.

Normally when I moved that bookcase, I had to take about half the books out because it was too heavy, but that day haste was the key word and I just picked up one side of it and swung it away from the wall. Once again, I jabbed the snake repeatedly with my shovel and killed him. Then I had to get a bucket and scoop him into it and take him outside. But at least I could go off and know it would be safe to come home from town. Tony didn't understand why I killed a "harmless" old gopher snake. In my book, the only good snake was a dead one.

The kitchen didn't have an oven, just a wood stove for heating water (and the house). But we had received a wedding gift from Tony's co-workers on the Philco job that certainly came in handy when I wasn't killing snakes. It was a Westinghouse electric roaster that people typically used for cooking a big turkey. The instructions said it could also be used for baking cakes, cookies, pies, casseroles, roasts, and meat loaf—and I got good with most of those. We bought a broiler attachment to go with it, so we could broil steak or hamburgers, and I found a two-burner electric hot plate in the closet. With these few appliances, I got along quite well and didn't even know that I was underprivileged—although I did gradually notice that none of the other young women that I knew lived quite the way we did.

Cooking like an American wife was important to me. Tony didn't even like to tell people we were Basque; he always said his family was Spanish, while admitting maybe mine was Basque. Even though we were poor, we did everything we could to fit in. We had already decided to speak only English with any children we would have. And we spent a lot of time in the winter of 1952 picking out very American-sounding names for the baby who was on the way. We were leading simple lives, but we wanted to take part in the American Dream all the same.

One of the first things we did was buy 50 baby chicks from Kent's. They cost $9.50 for the whole bunch. We got six hens from Tony's folks for $10.00 and some fertile eggs also. Mrs. Laca, a friend of my mother's, had a broody hen and we went over there at night and brought the hen home very cautiously in a closed box so she would not get over the notion that she wanted to raise chicks. We transferred her carefully to a dark chicken coop and put the fertile eggs under her. She stayed there taking good care of those eggs for 21 days. When they hatched, the chicks were so cute, and we were proud of the new additions.

Thus supplied, I went into the egg business and began to sell eggs to Kent's Grocery.

I bought an egg scale and a special cloth for cleaning them. You couldn't use water to clean them; Mr. Kent's rule, I guess. I averaged about five or six dozen eggs a week to sell. The price I got was 35 cents a dozen for small ones, 60 cents for medium, and 65 cents for large. The fringe benefit was that the chicken feed came in print cloth sacks instead of brown gunnysacks. When the sacks were emptied, I would take them apart and wash and iron them and then use them as fabric for sewing. I could make myself a sleeveless blouse with one sack, and a shirt for Tony took two.

The first thing I bought with my egg money was an end table which had little compartments on the ends for magazines. I bought it at a used furniture store for three dollars. We also read the classified ads in the paper and found a wringer-type washing machine for sale for thirty-five dollars. We bought that and set it up in the pump house with a drain to the ground outside. For the first few months, we heated water in the kitchen on the wood stove or, when the weather got hot, we gathered a circle of rocks outside, built a fire in the center, put a washtub on the rocks, and heated our water that way.

When 1952 dawned, we bought a hot water heater from Consumer's Supply, and this was installed in the pump house. I finally had hot water for laundry and dishes. We had rounded up a galvanized tub which was shaped like a bathtub (more or less) and it was more comfortable for baths than the round wash tub we had been using. And, of course, it was a real improvement over the outdoor shower. But we still hadn't finished the bathroom when it came time for me to give birth to my first child.

Unfortunately for Tony, I'd had enough of waiting around. One day in late April, I finished packing my bag to be ready for the trip to the hospital and left it by the wood box where we kept firewood for the stove. It had been in the same spot in that kitchen since I was kid. *I used to hide my dog in that box when strangers came to visit,* I thought as I set it down.

I had spent the day cleaning the house in a burst of energy I'd not felt in weeks. The baby was due any day, and I suppose my hormones had kicked in. They certainly had where my temper was concerned.

"If this bathroom isn't finished by the time the baby gets here, I am going straight from the hospital to my mother's house," I told Tony when he got home for lunch. He winced and grinned sheepishly.

"I know, I know, it's taking too long," Tony said, and promised to get Charlie Landis back at work right away.

I took Tony at his word, and as he usually did, he followed through. The next day, he drove me to the hospital to give birth—and, sure enough, we passed Charlie going the other direction on our trip into town. He was headed to our place.

I brought our daughter—christened with the solidly American name of Diane—home to the Belaustegui house and its brand-new bathroom!

ELADIA
Fallon, Nevada
August 1953

Eladia turned to the woman next to her and very carefully asked the question from the little booklet in her hand, *Twenty-Five Lessons in Citizenship*. She spoke slowly, struggling to form the words in English.

"Who was the first president of the United States?"

Consuela clapped her hands.

"Jorge Washing-tone!" she said with delight.

"*No es Jorge.* Gee-orge."

The correction came from the woman on Eladia's left. Celestina was a bit of a show-off.

"Yes, yes, George," said Consuela in English. Then in Spanish she added, "Eladia knew what I meant."

There was laughter all around, interrupted by a knock on the door.

Consuela, the hostess of this gathering, got up from her rose-colored velvet couch and walked to the door.

"*Vitori!*" she exclaimed when she found Victoria Rubianes standing at the door. "What's that you have? Look everyone, *Vitori* is here."

Victoria entered the room and exchanged greetings with the other women. In her arms she carried a large cardboard box.

"Have made cake," she announced in English.

Celestina and Eladia exchanged glances, Eladia looking the most confused until Celestina found the word in Spanish and translated.

"Oh, good, Consuela had only these few store-bought cookies," Eladia teased. There was more laughter.

"Ho, ho, ho! Like you are some bootlegger's wife!"

Consuela could give as good as she got.

Every other Sunday afternoon, the four women gathered at Consuela's house for coffee and to practice their English. They presented quite a class of learners. Eladia spoke no Basque, and Victoria spoke limited Spanish, while Celestina and Consuela passed back and forth between the two languages with relative ease. Despite Celestina's proclivity for correcting mistakes, Consuela spoke the most English. All of them laughed with equal ease.

Victoria had not yet been able to convince Eladia, who was "*sone kinda relayshun,*" due to her son having married Victoria's daughter, to at least think about American citizenship as well as her English skills. The naturalization process seemed overly complex and was not discussed in detail in the Sunday gatherings, but the four women did enjoy the experience of practicing their English without husbands and children and grandchildren underfoot. When there was cake, all the better.

"Let me get a knife for that cake," Consuela said. "Sit, sit!"

Celestina smirked. "Maybe you can cut down a cherry tree with the knife, like Jorge Washing-tone," she called after her friend.

Victoria, who had missed the earlier exchange and therefore the point of the joke, assumed her Spanish was failing her. She turned to Eladia and managed to ask, with words borrowed from all three languages being used in the room, how the Erquiagas were doing.

"We are still living with Jose Luis," Eladia said with a shrug. "I do not like that ranch, the Ernst place, because it is too close to the military base, and they have all those airplanes out there now. They fly over and scare my chickens! I never had blood spots in the eggs when we lived in Soda Lake, but they are a real problem at this ranch."

Celestina provided some translation and Victoria was soon able to agree.

"When we lived in that part of the valley, there were not as many planes," she said. "Blood in a chicken's egg is a sign of bad luck. Country living is hard. I am glad to live in town now and to be able to walk everywhere."

Victoria and Eladia shared a granddaughter, Diane, so they lapsed into multilingual conversation about how cute the one-year-old was. And then Consuela returned with the cake. The plate she handed Celestina had several cherries on it as well.

"Jorge says hello," she said with a smile.

***

Eladia took her time on the walk from Consuela's house to the Elks Lodge where she was to meet Marcelino. After dropping her off to sit with her friends, he had headed to the bar for a drink with a few other semi-retired men. Eladia was in no hurry to enter the smoke-filled Elks Lodge, and the varicose veins in her legs were hurting today, so a slow walk felt like the right thing to do.

Thirty-three years after her arrival in Nevada, Eladia was resigned to a life she had not so much chosen as accepted. With her children long since raised and living on their own—all but Trini and Louie were now married—her world seemed to grow smaller every year. She and Marcelino continued to live with one child or the other; they owned nothing but their car, clothing, and some household furnishings. Marcelino had his gophers to trap, and she had chickens to raise. It was not a hard life, but neither was it a particularly fulfilling one.

She knew the English lessons with her friends were the right thing to do, but she still resented the small-town life and American customs. Victoria might be headed for U.S. citizenship, but Eladia remained unconvinced that it was either necessary or possible; her English might never be good enough to survive the questions of a judge. *Still*, she thought as she turned the corner onto Maine Street, *maybe Victoria is right.* Maybe she needed to own something of her own, even if it was just a citizenship document.

A man approaching on the sidewalk tipped his hat as he caught Eladia's eye. Eladia smiled and nodded in return, hesitating just a moment.

"Good afternoon," she said in English just as the man passed by.

"Good afternoon, ma'am!" he called back over his shoulder.

Yes, maybe Victoria is right, she thought. *Perhaps it is time to give America a chance.*

Eladia stopped and leaned down to massage her legs for a few seconds, lost in thought. When she straightened up, she squared her shoulders just a little more than usual and proceeded on her way to meet Marcelino. She whispered to herself as she walked.

"George Washington became president of the United States in 1789."

VICTORIA
Fallon, Nevada
October 1954

Pushing her granddaughter's pram along the sidewalk always reminded Victoria of standing on the deck of the SS *La Touraine*, bound for America. She steamed boldly ahead, lost in thought. The older she got, the more she spent time in her mind reliving the past.

A man wearing overalls and a wide-brimmed straw hat nodded at Victoria from the doorway of one of the shops. He tipped his hat and mumbled a greeting.

"Hello!" Victoria called loudly as she slowed just a bit. When she had passed the man and the doorway, she redoubled her velocity.

"Who's that, Mom?"

Victoria remembered her daughter, Annie, was walking along beside her. She shrugged, keeping her eyes straight ahead as she responded.

"Don' know."

Annie laughed. "Mom, we have passed four people on the way to Kent's from your house, and every one of them has spoken to you. Don't you know any of them by name?"

"Why know names?" said Victoria. "Nice peoples."

Out of the corner of her eye, Victoria saw Annie shake her head. It was true, she didn't really know the good people of Fallon whom she passed every day on her way to run her errands. But she didn't mind. She enjoyed seeing people and being friendly. It gave her a sense of comfort, as if she no longer had to be quite so afraid.

Struggling to find the words in English, she switched to Basque.

"We lived out in the country for so many years when your father was alive," she explained. "You have to remember, when I was young, I lived in a small village, but we went into Lekeitio two or three times a month. Fallon reminds me of that."

"English, Mom," Annie scolded gently. "You should try to speak more English. The citizenship test will be given in English."

"I try," Victoria replied in English, nodding her head.

For over two years, Victoria had been studying for the citizenship exam. Her son, Bob, who until recently had continued to live with her, had helped, as had a few of the friends she knew around town. When Bob married Gert Jones and moved to a trailer park north of town, Annie took up the role of primary tutor to their mother. It was going reasonably well, but Victoria knew she wasn't ready for the test administration that would be given this month. She was planning to wait and present herself for citizenship in March 1955.

"How is baby?" she asked, changing the subject so she would not become nervous.

Annie touched the growing bump on her belly.

"Doctor says everything is just fine."

"Baby!" offered Diane from the bow of the SS *Victoria*.

"Yes, Diane. Baby." Annie laughed at her daughter's excitement. The two-year-old knew several words and had joyfully added "baby" to her vocabulary in the last few days.

"You will have a little brother or sister early next year," Annie said.

"Baby."

Another man, this one wearing a necktie with a crisp white shirt and dark trousers, stepped out of a storefront as the Rubianes women were passing.

"Well, hello there, Mrs. Rubianes!" he said.

"Hello," Victoria replied, coming to a stop. "Dis my daughter, Annie, and my...Diane." She gestured to Annie and the pram before her, at a loss for the word *granddaughter*.

The man exchanged greetings and bent to tickle Diane's cheek. He was reworded with a smile and another exclamation of "Baby!" He laughed and went his way.

"Who was that?" Annie teased.

"Don' know. I shop now. You go be big shot."

The two women shared a little laugh.

"Oh, Mom, I'm just off to the Republican Women's Club lunch. But thank you for letting me get out of the house. I'm sure Diane won't be any trouble. Have fun shopping!"

Annie headed up the street toward the Fallon Nugget, while Victoria and the baby entered the store by way of the door the man had just exited. Once inside, Victoria leaned down close to her granddaughter.

"Your mother is going to be an important person," she said in Basque, her smile big enough to cause the baby to smile back.

ANNIE
Fallon, Nevada
March 1955

America had two new citizens.

My mother and mother-in-law had both passed their citizenship exam with, as my favorite teacher Anne Gibbs used to say, flying colors. All their English lessons paid off as they each answered Judge Frank Gregory's questions in a calm but forceful way—just as they had lived their entire lives.

Eladia wore a hat her daughters had purchased for the occasion: black velvet with a bow on the side. It sat back on her graying hair and framed her face beautifully. Mom's hair, which was dyed a dark shade of brown, was covered with one of her signature hairnets. My brother's Purple Heart medal from the war was pinned to the lapel of her jacket. Both women almost glimmered with an inner light, they were so proud.

The courthouse had been full an hour before the ceremony was scheduled to begin. Family and friends gathered, introduced themselves, and laughed and smiled while they waited for the judge to arrive. The many languages spoken made the place sound like the United Nations must, because, truth be told, America didn't have just two new citizens. Seven people—six women and one man—answered Judge Gregory's questions that day and later swore the oath that made them Americans: two from England, one from China, one from Finland, one from the Philippines, and of course our two from Spain.

Miss Rosalind Weyant, one of the BPW ladies who organized the ceremony and the reception that followed, gave a talk about the United States Constitution. I was too choked up to hear what she said, but I'm sure it was grand. Judge Gregory gave a little welcoming address as well.

During the reception, my father-in-law Marcelino beamed with pride as he squired Eladia around the room, introducing his favorite new American to all and sundry. She clung to him like a bird on a branch, and it was truly the most I think I'd ever seen her smile. I felt bad that Mom was on her own, and I wished my father could have lived to see this day. But for the ten years since Pop died, Mom had been more than a wife, more than a widow. She was her own person. She had lived out the dreams of that little girl with the chestnut hair whose story she used to tell me when I was a kid at the Bassett Ranch.

I was standing by the wall when former Assemblyman George Frey came over to chat.

"George, how nice of you to be here!" I said. "How's Elenor?"

"She's good, and you know I wouldn't have missed this for the world. I may not miss being in the legislature, but I do miss seeing this kind of ceremony. This is America in action."

I agreed with him and said something silly like, "Well said, George." I never was very eloquent.

What he said in reply bowled me over.

"The Republican Party is looking for candidates to run for the legislature next year, particularly women. All this business with school reform and taxes has turned the political world upside down, and frankly the men in charge have made a mess of things. We'll lose both of Churchill County's seats in the assembly if we're not careful." He paused and looked at me.

"I think you should run for my old seat, Speed."

I was surprised he used my old nickname. Nobody outside the family did anymore. But I was even more surprised by his suggestion I run for office. I'd been attending a few meetings, and Tony and I were active with Farm Bureau, but this was something else entirely. My surprise must have shown on my face because George's eyes got wide.

"Can we still you call you that?" he asked.

"I wish you wouldn't," I said with a laugh. "I've got two kids now and I'm moving pretty slowly these days." I pointed over to where Diane and her new baby brother, Steve, were sitting with my sister. George laughed along with me. I hesitated before tackling the real surprise.

"You know, it's not nice to tease an old married woman about things like running for office, George. I'm a housewife."

George shook his head.

"I'm not teasing you, *Anita,*" he said, nodding for emphasis as he pronounced my name. "Not one bit. You'd make a fine candidate, and a fine assemblyman."

"Oh, George, I'm not sure I even make a fine wife and mother, let alone an assemblyman. Or assemblywoman, I guess."

We both laughed at that. George gestured at my mother and mother-in-law, both of whom had a glass of punch by that point and were toasting the five other new Americans in the corner.

"I think all those people over there might think differently," George said. "They might say it was the whole point of today. And two of them would say it was the whole point of them coming here from Spain in the first place."

I didn't know what to say to that. George left his words hanging and turned to walk away. I was still trying to think of something to say when he turned back around.

"Just promise me you'll think about it?" he asked. "Sure, sure, I will," I stammered after him as he walked away.

"And . . . George! Thank you for thinking of me." He smiled and gestured with his hand as if tipping his hat in my direction. Then he was gone.

***

By the time summer rolled around, political talk was heating up. The legislature made sweeping changes to the public education system that year, following a lot of work Governor Russell and others had been doing on school finance and related issues. People were mad on both sides, and there was more and more talk about finding new candidates for the next election. My Republican Women's Club lunches got a lot more interesting!

At home, I had my hands full with two young children, my egg business, and feeding Tony and the work crews he hired to help during the hay season. When I broached the subject of running for office, Tony got a pained look on his face that I knew meant he didn't want to discuss the topic.

A couple of my girlfriends from high school had married local farmers and settled down, just like I had, so I turned to them for advice. We conspired over coffee and reminisced about the "good old days" when we thought we ran Churchill County High School. I even talked to my friend Ivy in Carson City. She and her husband still ran in the political circles where I'd cut my teeth as a young clerk at the Employment Security Department.

The women were all for me running, but they also said it probably couldn't be done successfully. No matter how angry people said they were about public education, taxes, and politics, women didn't get elected to very many jobs.

And I could tell I was changing. Annie, the little Basque girl who didn't have a care in the world, had moved on to become a wife and mother. There were fewer and fewer opportunities to go out and dance and socialize, so the friendly and outgoing Annie who loved political dinners in Carson City became more and more a stay-at-home housewife. The idea of a campaign scared me, to be honest.

My mother, who had always seemed to be afraid of everything and lived by the rules of her superstitions, was surprisingly the biggest champion.

"Why you think we come to America?" she asked in her steadily improving English. "Yes, Pop and me wanted better jobs for us. But more we wanted better life for our kids."

She sounded a lot like George Frey had at the naturalization ceremony. Maybe this was the whole point of our American experience? It dawned on me at long last that my mother's superstitions were less about fear and more about ways to order her world—to control things she didn't understand because she didn't have the benefit of an education. Or, if she couldn't control them, she could at least explain them.

I thought, too, about my mother-in-law, Eladia. The woman never smiled except when her children were gathered around her living room and Spanish flowed freely. Where my own mother held her world together with superstition and rules, Eladia seemed to move through life with some combination of ignorance and bliss. I never knew what was going on in her head. She was always so quiet and, I still thought after all these years, somehow *resigned*. Resigned to playing the hand she'd been dealt. Did I want that life for myself? Or did I want to prove my mother right and take a risk?

I wouldn't have the answer until Christmas.

Since we'd finished remodeling the Belaustegui house in 1952, my brothers and sisters and their spouses gathered at our place for Christmas Eve. I only had one niece (Jessie's daughter, Judy), and since Mom and my brothers lived in Fallon, ours was the logical gathering place. I loved the Christmas season. I'd bought a Nativity scene with some of my egg money, and as Diane got old enough, I loved telling her the Bible story and getting her to help me set up the statues of the Holy Family and the Three Wise Men. My brother Tony continued to play Santa Claus each year, as he had when I was young; I think he loved it as much as the kids!

We weren't big drinkers, but my siblings and their spouses were inclined to have a few shots of whiskey during the holidays, so things got more and more lively as the night's festivities wore on. Inevitably, my brother-in-law George had one too many and started offering his opinion about politics. The conversation got pretty heated. I was sort of enjoying the give and take, and then I noticed that familiar pained expression on my husband's face. Before long, he excused himself and went outside, ostensibly to check on the cows. Watching him go, I wondered whether, if I ran for the legislature, my marriage could withstand first the life of a candidate, then me being gone for several months every other year, busy with work in Carson City.

While I was washing up some glasses in the kitchen, my sister Jessie joined me.

"What's this talk of you running for office?" she asked. Her tone wasn't encouraging.

I tried to laugh it off.

"Oh, you must have been talking to Mom," I said. "It's just gossip in town."

"Well, good," came her reply. "I'm glad it's only gossip. You've got two kids to raise. I had my hands full just running the sewing store and raising Judy – and you know, we couldn't make that work."

My sister and her husband had tried their hand as the owners of a sewing and craft supplies store in Hawthorne but had closed the business because it was just too hard to make ends meet. I remember thinking, as I stared at the last glass in the sink, that maybe she was right. When Tony came back in from outside, the expression still apparent on his face underscored what I'd been thinking.

We bundled the kids off to bed and then all the women went to Midnight Mass, while the menfolk stayed at home to play cards. I dropped Mom at her place in town, drove home, and crawled into bed. Tony was already asleep, and the others were long gone. I must have fallen into a deep sleep because the next thing I knew, the phone ringing in the kitchen woke me up and I was running to answer. It was my sister.

"We're at the hospital," Polly said. "Mom's had a stroke."

Apparently, Polly and George had stopped by my mother's house for breakfast and found her unconscious on the floor of her tiny kitchen.

"They think it was fairly minor, but the doctor won't say much, other than that we should expect more strokes as she ages. We're wondering if she will be able to live alone. It's going to take a while to sort all that out."

And, just like that, I understood what it meant to lose control of the rules and resign yourself to a less risky life. I called George Frey two days later and told him to find another candidate.

PART SEVEN:

Endings

1963–1972

VICTORIA
August 4, 1963
Reno, Nevada

The woman with hair the color of granite lay in solitude, her eyes closed. Today, like most days, she slept soundly, her breathing the only sign of life. She had not spoken in several days.

Victoria Rubianes, age 80, was no longer in communication with the world around her. Her children and grandchildren sometimes came and went from her hospital room, but she rarely acknowledged them. After several small strokes that slowly robbed her of the ability to live on her own, a massive cerebral hemorrhage in July sent her to Saint Mary's Hospital, unable to speak, walk, or feed herself. Now when she did open her eyes, they often filled with tears.

Her mind remained active, however—something the doctors and nurses only guessed at. "Squeeze her hand," they advised her children. "Talk to her."

But Victoria did not respond. She was thinking of Victor and Manuel, her husband and oldest son who had crossed over to Heaven before her. She wanted to see them again. She hoped that her father and mother would be waiting for her, too. In her mind, she gripped her father's pocket watch and prepared for the journey. Today, she knew, was the end.

ANNIE
August 4, 1963
Fallon, Nevada

I had the good fortune of having a private room at Churchill Public Hospital. The oppressive summer heat, breaking records that year, had apparently driven most illnesses, births, and even deaths away. The hospital was nearly empty. I was relieved to have the peace and quiet of my room, something I never had in the home I shared with Tony and our three children. We had sent the kids camping with my brother Tony and his wife Van, but I was still enjoying the time away from the ranch. There was still so much work to be done on the new house we had moved onto our own land. My back hurt from all the painting and my temper was short. *A wife and mother deserves this brief respite*, I thought.

A noise at the door caught my attention. I glanced over, barely moving my head on the pillow, to see my brother, Bob, standing in the hallway just outside. Sunlight streamed from the windows and illuminated his face in a way I found beautiful. Or maybe it was the drugs the nurse had just given me for the pain . . .   "You look like an angel," I whispered.

Bob took a few steps into the room, swinging his one good leg on his crutches. As he moved out of the direct sunlight, I could see he had been crying.

"Oh," I sighed. "An angel of death, then. You're here to tell me Mom died, aren't you?"

Bob nodded but didn't speak. He completed his journey across the hospital room, coming to a stop by the bed, and reached out to grasp my hand.

"Are you okay?"

I laughed, a short staccato sound with a hint of sarcasm. Silence followed.

"Yes, I'm okay," I finally said. "I knew Mom didn't have long to live. I've had one of her famous 'feelings' all week, but I just hoped it wouldn't be today. What kind of a birthday is it for a grandchild to enter the world at the same time their grandmother leaves it? Mom would have a field day with superstitions about why this is a terrible idea."

I relaxed a little and chuckled, more warmly this time. Bob took a breath, but then he laughed with me. Silence fell again.

Then, there was a soft knock at the door.

"Mrs. Erquiaga? It's time."

Bob turned and in the same motion stepped to one side so I could see the door. A nurse was waiting there.

"Okay," I said without enthusiasm.

"Your drugs should have kicked in by now, so we're going to take you into delivery. It's time to get that baby out of you!" The nurse seemed awfully chipper.

I sighed and turned my face to the wall. My thoughts ventured inward, remembering scenes from my childhood on the porch of the Bassett place, and more recent times, before my mother's illness, laughing at life's little events and Mom's wry sense of humor. I remembered last Christmas, before the big stroke, when Mom had yet again insisted on eating in the kitchen because thirteen people had arrived for dinner, and everyone knew that was bad luck.

I chuckled again and looked back at Bob.

"She really would have a field day with this timing, you know."

***

Back then, doctors kept you in the hospital for several days after childbirth, so I couldn't even attend Mom's funeral. From the phone at my bedside, I helped make the arrangements to have her buried next to my father at the Churchill County Cemetery. And I made sure Tony took the kids to the service.

"Why don't we get one of my sisters to watch them?" he had complained when I phoned to tell him I wanted all three kids to attend the funeral. "Carl is only six, for heaven's sake."

"It's good for them to learn about death," I had pushed back. "I was only 16 when Pop died, and I walked around in a daze because I'd never been to a funeral."

I won in the end, of course. I usually did with Tony. Ever since I had given up much of a life outside our home when I decided not to run for office, he left most of the decisions about raising the kids to me. Although I'd never been around children before we had ours, I quickly learned the ropes and quite enjoyed being a mother.

Still, I knew my world was getting smaller and smaller with each passing year. The outgoing girl of my youth had become more of an introvert and spent most of her time at home or with a few close friends. Church played a role in my life, as did the Republican Women's Club, but my family took precedence. I turned more and more to arts and crafts as an outlet, and there was plenty of work to do making our new house a home.

We'd bought a run-down old duplex from the military in late 1962 and had moved it to some land we bought behind the Belaustegui place. I'd spend the months leading up to the birth of our fourth child remodeling and fixing it up. Charlie Landis, who'd been so helpful with the old house in 1952, was called back into service. Thanks to his talents and my S&H Green Stamps, I had added a few special touches to the house: A clock with a carving of Mount Vernon on it. A shelf for knickknacks over the kitchen counter. A built-in laundry hamper for the kids' bathroom. It was mighty high living, compared to the old Belaustegui house. It was good to have a place of our own, and I looked forward to continuing to host my family for Christmas—and maybe we'd invite all the Erquiagas over for New Year's Day from now on.

"Be sure my sister remembers to bury Mom with her father's pocket watch," I told Tony as I hung up the phone and turned to the nurse who was waiting to poke and prod my stomach to be sure I was healing.

"I wish my husband was as well behaved as yours," the nurse said with a smile. "It's not easy being a wife and mother, is it?"

That made me think of the life Mom had lived. Had it been hard for her? I don't remember her complaining. True, she'd never seemed to have much time for me when I was little. My father and I were much closer. But after Pop died, my mother and I were all each other had. We became good friends. When I had kids of my own, she had always been there for me—and them. Singing to them in Basque, worrying in her superstitious ways. Now she was gone. The world felt a little bit smaller. I felt a little more alone, and I resolved to find ways to keep her memory alive. Maybe someday I'll write a story about her . . .

ELADIA
May 1971
Fallon, Nevada

The three Erquiaga boys squirmed and wiggled nervously on the bed. Aged 16, 14, and 8, their demeanor made it clear they would have preferred to be almost anywhere but in a hospital room with their grandmother, mother, and aunt.

"How come Diane didn't have to come?" Carl, the middle son, had whined in the car on the way into town.

"Your sister is off with her boyfriend, planning their wedding, and you know that very well," their mother, Anita, had replied, her tone curt and her voice just a bit too loud for how close the boys were sitting to her in the family station wagon.

No one had spoken for the rest of the drive. These trips to visit their grandmother, Eladia, after she had broken her leg in a fall at home and subsequently suffered a stroke during the months of recovery, were a regular occurrence. Sometimes the boys' mother drove them alone; sometimes their father came to see his mother.

Today, at least, the boys' Aunt Trini was present in the hospital room. That helped with the awkward silences. Their grandmother had spoken only a few words of English before the stroke. She was even less communicative afterward.

On the empty hospital bed in the room designed for two patients, quiet so as not to draw attention to themselves, the boys stared at the floor and fidgeted, fighting for space on the crisp white sheets and neatly folded light blue blanket. Eladia slept in the other bed, just a few feet away. Trini and their mother sat together by the window and talked in hushed tones. Steve was lightly punching his brothers on the arm, trying to entertain himself, and perhaps them. The youngest boy, Dale, kept staring at his grandmother. Her open mouth and heavy breathing scared him so much it seemed best to keep a constant eye on her.

In her sleep, Eladia's right hand skirred across the blanket, her fingers moving rapidly up and down, back and forth.

"She's playing the piano," Trini said, as much to herself as to Anita or the boys. "In her mind, I think she's playing the piano."

Suddenly, Eladia's eyes were open.

"Mom!" Dale called. "She's awake!"

Trini and Anita both stood up. Trini spoke to her mother in Spanish, words the boys did not understand. Eladia looked puzzled for a moment, then glanced around the room.

"Get up, boys, so she can see you," their mother said. The boys obliged.

Eladia instantly became animated. Even with her left side almost motionless, she tried to sit up in bed, and she spoke rapidly in Spanish.

"*Niños, mis niños! Vámanos, vámanos!*" She carried on for a few more sentences and then slumped back in the bed, visibly spent.

Trini looked shocked for a moment. Then she spoke to her mother, who shook her head and uttered a few more sentences, in what sounded to the boys and their mother like an angry tone. After a pause, Trini laughed a little to herself and turned to her sister-in-law.

"Well, I don't understand this at all, but I guess it's part of her stroke. She thinks the boys are her children—me and Pilar and Joe, I guess. She's saying 'Children, we are going, we are going.' And she's talking about El Jardín . . ." Trini's voice trailed off.

"El Jardín?" asked Anita.

"It means 'the garden,'" Trini replied. "But it's also the name of a house in Spain. She took us there when we were kids, maybe once or twice. A rich old woman lived there. I think she was some kind of royalty." Trini paused, shaking her head. "I just don't understand."

Anita seemed to grasp what was going on.

"Past lives," she said. "Or rather, reliving the one she had. Playing the piano, visiting old houses. Something similar happened with my mother, too. The brain plays tricks. Memories get jumbled."

Trini nodded and stared at the woman in the bed.

"I haven't thought of that place in years," she said quietly. Then she said something to her mother in Spanish.

"*Sí, sí, vámanos!*" Eladia urged. She looked at the boys and smiled the biggest smile any of them could ever remember seeing from her.

"*Vámanos,*" she said again.

ANNIE
February 1972
Fallon, Nevada

The Fallon Mortuary smelled of formaldehyde and lilies, a sickening but all-too-familiar assault on the senses. As I sat with my family in a dark room behind the alcove where the casket containing my mother-in-law's body was displayed, I forced myself to count how many times I had smelled this place, how many funerals I had attended here. Pop, Uncle Pete, my brother Tony, two of my husband's uncles, his sister-in-law and her baby, a few friends lost too early, and even the local parish priest. I had to smile at this last memory, recalling how much my kids had complained when I took them to the priest's funeral as "practice" for the day when someone close to them would die. Maybe I spent too much time thinking about funerals?

It soon became apparent that my youngest son, Dale, clearly needed more practice in the art of public grief, however. He was swinging his feet as the Rosary was chanted by the mourners gathered around us. I kept reaching down to rest my hand on his knee so he would stop moving.

Occasionally I looked over at my father-in-law, Marcelino. He seemed broken. A short man, tonight he looked even tinier, as if he were trying to shrink into his chair. Eladia had been ill for nearly two years, living out her life in hospitals and rest homes, but her poor husband still seemed shocked by her death. Or just overwhelmed, maybe. It made me sad.

Eladia had not been the warmest person, but she was unfailingly kind to me—treated me like an equal, or at least like one of her own daughters. She refused to speak English whenever we visited, even though I didn't understand much Spanish.

"Mama, she doesn't understand you!" my sisters-in-law would say when they caught their mother prattling away at me in Spanish over coffee at her kitchen table.

"She understands me fine," Eladia would reply.

I understood enough Spanish to get the message. And I had to give the woman credit for sticking to her guns. She had been tough, that much was certain. Probably tougher than any of us really knew.

As the mourners moved from one prayer to the next, I looked back and forth between my father-in-law and my husband. Both had tears in their eyes.

Who says the men are the strong ones? I remember thinking. And I thought back to my wedding rehearsal dinner and the toast I'd offered as a young bride. "To the wives," I'd said then. And I still believed they deserved the recognition.

I guess neither my mother nor my mother-in-law led overly exciting lives. They were simple people, really. But they'd been the glue that held their families together, just as I'd been doing since I married Tony and we started our lives together. Sure, none of us was famous, and we weren't winning any awards (unless you counted the number of eggs sold or the vegetables displayed at the county fair). But our families were healthy and happy, and who knew what the next generation might accomplish? Hadn't that been the point, just as Mom had once told me? The future generations?

Just then, Dale resumed swinging his feet, interrupting my train of thought. I reached down to tap his knee again.

"Knock it off," I whispered, but I softened the scolding with a smile and a wink. "Pay attention. You might learn something important."

EPILOGUE

June 24, 2004
Fallon, Nevada

Annie's husband died on February 6, 2004. Despite the fact that Tony had been ill for three months, Annie was caught completely off guard. When her children came home from the hospital to tell her their father would not recover from his recent illness and that they intended to bring him home for hospice care until the end, she stared at them incredulously.

"But I was supposed to die first," she declared. "Your father always told me he would live to be a hundred."

Exhausted by the realization that this eventuality was not in the cards, and worn down by years of poor health, Annie spent the months following Tony's death in an uncomfortable limbo, trying to come to terms with widowhood and a life she had never expected to lead. She marked the time by keeping track of her blood sugar, her diabetes seeming to take center stage as the most important actor in her life.

On June 19, one of Annie's granddaughters was married in a ceremony at her parents' ranch. Annie donned a brightly colored pantsuit and sallied forth (as she was wont to say), happy to have all her children and most of her grandchildren around her. When her youngest son said goodbye to her the next day and headed back to his home in Las Vegas, she got tears in her eyes and pointed to a bag of political paraphernalia she had collected over the years.

"If anything happens to me," she said, "be sure to take that. You're the only one who'd want it." She did not need to add that the bag represented a life unlived, a life spent watching others succeed in politics and underscoring the fact that she had never run for office, never had more titles than wife, mother, and grandmother. Her son knew, and he took the bag.

Three days later, Annie sat before the hand-me-down computer given to her by her middle son and put some finishing touches on the stories she had been writing. Over the years, with the help of her sister, Annie had collected tales of her family and of Tony's. She had written down everything she could remember about her own life as well, and hers was the story she was still polishing, editing it over and over.

She stared at the screen.

This is the story of Annie. Annie was a little Basque girl, born to Victoria and Victor Rubianes in Fallon, Nevada in 1928. She was the youngest of six children.

Annie was christened "Anita May Rubianes" at the Catholic Church in Austin, but, as far back as she can remember, her mother and father called her Annie. She was called Speed, Anita, Mother, and Granny by her siblings, friends, children, and grandchildren over the years. But when she sat down and really thought about it, she liked the name Annie best. In her memory, it was associated with the closeness and nurturing that comes with parental love. Those years of living at home as Annie were the years that molded the person she turned out to be.

She was a happy person who didn't have to work very hard, as some of her siblings apparently did. She had next to nothing of monetary value during her growing-up years, although she didn't know it at the time. She was outgoing and friendly and was not timid about doing anything in school. Somehow, her "old country" parents managed to instill in her a sense of self-worth.

Who is this person, Annie? Well, I, Anita Erquiaga, am Annie. I am writing about my life, hoping that someday my children and grandchildren will read this story and learn something from it. I turned out to be a history buff, so I hope there will be something of historical interest in this story . . . and maybe a few laughs along the way. It was a

good life. My only claim to fame is my children and
grandchildren. I'm very proud of all of them and I
feel no one could leave a better legacy.

Satisfied, she printed the final pages and switched off the computer. She turned out the light and went to sit at the kitchen counter to wait for some of her grandkids, who were coming for dinner. Once the youngsters had come and gone, with a few happy tales exchanged during the meal, Annie retired to bed in the same room where her husband of 54 years had passed away.

She died in her sleep.

Made in the USA
Middletown, DE
07 May 2022

65347374R00136